The Walker on the Cape

Cover Photo:
Grand Bank Lighthouse reprinted
by permission from the blog
"Recollections of a Vagabonde" -
http://avagabonde.blogspot.com.

The Walker on the Cape

Mike Martin

Dedication

To Jonathan and Sarah. I am very proud of you and the people you have become.

Acknowledgements

I would like to thank a number of people for helping me get Windflower out of my head and onto the pages of this book. They include early readers like Lynne and Joan who made many worthwhile suggestions to guide me on this journey. Later readers like Andy and my editorial guide Ruth Latta also helped me re-focus and eventually look smarter. And the constant love and support of my partner, Joan, who really did make all of this possible.

Finally to the wonderful people and scenery of Newfoundland which was the inspiration for all of this creation. I am grateful to the weather, yes even the fog which may block the sun but also keeps us safe and certainly gives us something to talk and write about.

Chapter One

Even in an ordinary life the most extraordinary things can happen. Every morning for the past eleven years Elias Martin had his breakfast of hot porridge and thick molasses bread smothered in partridgeberry jam. Then, rain or shine, he began his solitary walk from his small blue house on Elizabeth Avenue in Grand Bank, Newfoundland, down through the Cove, and until the winter snow made it impassable, up over the hills to the Cape.

This solitary pilgrimage allowed him to mourn his wife Eileen without anyone intruding on his grief. More importantly, it allowed him to talk to her without anyone thinking he was crazier than he was. This walk was one that they had shared for almost forty years until she took sick and he still missed her and still needed to feel her comforting presence. He thought that her long, painful, and ultimately fatal battle with cancer would be the worst part of his life. Now he knew that being without her was even worse.

People along the coastline in Grand Bank could set their clocks by Elias Martin. Every morning, even when the fog floated in from Fortune, they saw his hunched figure climb and disappear in the mist that ran the shoreline like a rum runner. You could put a pot of soup on to boil when he set out and be sure that when he appeared again that the potatoes, carrots, and turnips would be soft and sweet.

Mavis Emberly was one such soup-maker who relied on Elias Martin to set the pace for her weekly batch of pea soup. "There he goes," she remarked to her husband, Francis, "Time to put the soup on".

An hour and a half later Francis Emberly muttered, "Something's burning in that kitchen, maid." Mrs. Emberly ran to the kitchen to turn off her black bottomed soup with a smattering of non-religious but surely immoral curses and immediately realized that something else was wrong besides her spoiled soup. Elias hadn't returned. "Or else I missed him," she decided.

It wasn't until the next morning that the rest of the world discovered what her burnt pot of pea soup had already signaled. Elias Martin was found stone cold dead by a pair of hiking tourists, lying silently on the well-trod path that he and Eileen had travelled together for so many years.

"A heart attack" was what all the neighbours told themselves as they huddled over coffee at the local café and rumour mill. "A stroke" was whispered by the church ladies as they left the garden party planning meeting at the Anglican Church. But even as the now late Elias Martin's body lay on a cold slab at the local clinic, some of them suspected that something or someone else had been involved in the death of the solitary walker. The only one who knew for sure was Elias Martin and he sure wasn't talking. Who would finally unravel the mystery of the Walker on the Cape?

Chapter Two

That task would fall to the local gendarme, headed by Sergeant Winston Windflower of the Royal Canadian Mounted Police. Windflower was a full-blooded Cree from the Pink Lake Reserve in Northern Alberta who had been on assignment in Grand Bank for just over a year. He was worried about handling his first big case in this small Newfoundland community but it sure seemed a welcome break from chasing the teenagers who had taken to drinking beer underneath the wharf every warm night during the spring and summer.

"So where do we begin, Sarge?" asked Constable Eddie Tizzard. Tizzard, the local boy made good, was excited at his chance to show the townsfolk that he had more than the shiny red serge and polished brown boots working for him.

"Easy, Constable," said Windflower. "We have to make sure we get this right. Let's start at the beginning. Talk to the tourists who found Mr. Martin and then head over to see Doc Sanjay at the clinic. If it was a heart attack or stroke he should be able to verify that for us and we can wrap this up by lunchtime."

Tizzard almost said "I hope not," but judging by the stern look on his Sergeant's face he rethought that strategy and simply said "Sure thing, Boss," grabbed his hat and headed out the door.

Windflower wasn't sure it was a heart attack either. Something gnawed at his gut that told him there was more to this story than a simple coronary failure. But he kept his own counsel and simply nodded to his eager subordinate as he left the office. He decided to head over to the best source of informal information, the Mug-Up Café, for a cup of strong black tea and a snoop around.

"Morning, Sheila," he called as he spied the owner of the café struggling to balance three mugs of coffee and multiple orders of thick, home-made toast.

"Morning, Sergeant," Sheila smiled, blushing a little from the exertion of her load but more from the sight of this dashing young Mountie. Something about a man in uniform, she thought.

"A cup of tea when you get a chance," he said, returning her smile. That was pleasant, he thought to himself, and then just as quickly put his official game face back on. This was no time to give the regulars any reason to doubt his professionalism.

Windflower settled into a small table near the counter, a great place to watch everyone who came and went, but more importantly the best location to gently eavesdrop on the hushed conversations that were happening in every corner of the café. They had all seen him come in but he had learned that people's basic need to gossip overcame almost all of their other emotions, especially if they have a juicy piece of news to share with their fellow gossip-mongers. Sheila had just brought his steaming mug of tea with an added twinkle when his cell phone rang.

Every eye in the place turned on him at once as he asked the café owner if he could take the call in her small office at the back.

"Sure, Sergeant, anything for the Mounties," said Sheila, beaming.

Windflower hurried to the back and spoke to his constable. "What's up, Tizzard?"

"Sarge, I think you should come over to the clinic and hear what the Doc has to say for himself," said Tizzard.

"Stay right there, Tizzard, I'm on my way," said Windflower.

Chapter Three

Sergeant Windflower slurped a few gulps of his tea, waved goodbye to Sheila and took off for his patrol car, leaving a cool breeze and hot murmurings in his wake. Sheila followed him with her eyes all the way out, admiring not only the trim cut of his uniform but his tall, proud and erect posture as he started his car and headed out. For his part Windflower was still smiling from the warm welcome that Sheila Hillier had given him along with his tea this morning.

Sheila was a fiery red-headed born and bred Newfoundlander who had started the Mug-Up after the sudden loss of her husband in a heavy equipment accident in Fort McMurray. Maybe it was the northern Alberta connection that first attracted him to her. No, it was definitely her long sleek legs and her soft, yet honest sensuality. That's quite a woman, he thought. But he couldn't let himself go there, at least not yet.

He pulled into the cramped parking lot of the Grand Bank clinic and moved quickly to get out of the deadening mist that would soon cover the entire peninsula. He nodded to Tizzard who was sitting in the waiting room chatting to the receptionist, Betty Halliday, who liked nothing better than to be charmed by a man in uniform, any uniform.

"He's with somebody, Sarge," said Tizzard, who blushed a little when he saw his superior, but still managed a sly smile back to Betty Halliday who glowed even pinker than ever.

Just then Doctor Vinjay Sanjay came out of his office, with his arms around the shoulders of an elderly patient who probably needed company more than medical attention.

"Good Morning Sergeant Windflower," said the short, bespectacled and slightly stooped doctor. "How's she going by?" he laughingly asked.

Windflower laughed at the combination of Indian formality and newly acquired Newfie lingo. He replied as he always did with "Great, how's my favourite Indian on the South Coast?" Both of the men laughed again at their inside joke.

"Come in, come in," said Doctor Sanjay, realizing that the time for joking was over.

"So what have we got?" asked Windflower as soon as the door was closed.

"Well as I was explaining to your constable here there was no outward sign of trauma on the body and most of the locals could be forgiven for thinking that this chap died of a heart attack. In fact he did have a massive coronary failure. But when I examined Mr. Martin I noticed a few irregularities that do not normally present in an acute heart attack."

"What do you mean, Doc?" asked Windflower.

"Well, come with me and I'll show you," said the doctor.

He led Windflower and the surprisingly quiet Tizzard into a small refrigerated back room that served as the make-shift morgue for the clinic. He pulled back the sheet covering the remains of Elias Martin that by now was graying and frozen stiff in rigor mortis. Both Windflower and Tizzard were taken aback by the sour cloying smell of death but Doctor Sanjay seemed completely unaffected by his surroundings.

"You see here, Sergeant, that when I pull on this man's fingernails they come completely off and it's the same with his toenails. Usually they would be rock-solidly attached to the deceased. And you can pull his hair off in clumps," he said, clutching a wad of the dead man's hair in his fist. "It seemed strange so I sent a hair and blood sample to a friend in the lab in St. John's by taxi last night and I just got the call back before Constable Tizzard arrived."

"So, what is it?" asked Windflower.

"He's been poisoned, Sarge," blurted out Tizzard, unable to hold back any longer.

"Is that right, Doc?" asked Windflower. "Poisoned? Could it have been an accident?"

"Not likely. Otherwise my waiting room would be full of people suffering from poisoning. As strange as it may seem, Sergeant, this man died of a massive coronary failure that seemed to have been directly related to acute arsenic poisoning. I've never seen a case like this before personally but the evidence appears quite clear. Elias Martin died directly as a result of arsenic poisoning and given the amount in his system it was likely administered over a long period of time. How it got there I haven't a clue. But I guess that's your job, Sergeant Windflower."

"I guess it is," said Windflower softly.

Chapter Four

Well, you asked for something interesting to happen, thought Windflower, but arsenic poisoning? Never in a million years!

After swearing Tizzard to total secrecy at the risk of two weeks straight on the solitary midnight shift, he headed back to the scene of Elias Martin's death to contemplate his next move. When he pulled his car up to the base of the trail the Cape was still draped in the last gasps of morning fog that would soon be burnt off by the sun and swept out to sea. He needed time and space to think.

As he stared up at the trail he thought about the basics of a murder investigation that he had learned at the RCMP training school in Regina. Motive, means, and opportunity were the keys. But was Elias Martin's death really a murder? So far he had little of anything except a dead body with signs of poisoning. That might be the means but who would have any reason to kill a seventy-two year old man and who would have had the opportunity to kill a man who lived alone and apparently socialized very little?

As the fog lifted Windflower's course of action became clearer as well. "We'll treat the death of Elias Martin as suspicious, without revealing anything else," he thought to himself. "That should shake up the locals a bit and maybe the guilty party will make some kind of move that will bring him out into the open."

He climbed back into his car and called Constable Tizzard on his police radio, knowing that the police frequency was regularly monitored by a couple of local busy bodies who would help spread the information he was about to reveal to Tizzard.

"Tizzard, based on the information we received this morning we are going to treat Elias Martin's death as suspicious. I need you to interview all the neighbours and, as much as possible, reconstruct his daily routines. Also, I want to know if he had any close friends or confidants. And most importantly, I want to know if he had any enemies or anybody who he may have pissed off, even if it was a long time ago. Memories are long in a small community."

"Okay, Sarge, I'll head over to see the neighbours this morning," replied Tizzard.

"Great, we'll check in later. Over and out."

That should get things moving, thought Windflower. We'll use the rumour mill and good old fashioned police work at the same time. As Windflower headed back to the detachment he was still puzzled by what he had just learned about the death of Elias Martin, but at least he had the beginnings of a plan.

Now he had to start the dreaded paperwork that accompanied any major investigation and even worse he had to call his superior, Inspector MacIntosh in Marystown.

For nearly a year now he had avoided the scrutiny of his Boss, mostly because there had been little to report from Grand Bank other than the petty crime and motor vehicle accidents that were the regular routine of police work in a small community. So far he had stayed out of MacIntosh's line of fire, but that was about to change in a hurry.

Windflower made the call but as luck would have it, MacIntosh was out of town in St. John's at an anti-drug symposium.

Great, that gives me at least a few days to find some evidence, he thought. Maybe I can find a motive and opportunity as well.

Chapter Five

While Tizzard was checking out the neighbours Windflower decided to make his own visit to the late Elias Martin's house to take a look around for himself. He also wanted to make sure that no one tampered with any evidence in the old man's home.

The curtains were drawn as he pulled into the gravel driveway of the small blue house on Elizabeth Avenue. None of the neighbours seemed to be around which suited Windflower just fine; let Tizzard deal with their nosiness and questions. Soon enough the word would spread that the Mounties were at the Martin house and that should get the rumours going and maybe shake out a few shreds of truth at the same time.

The old wooden house was sparse but clean. Martin must have had a cleaning lady, Windflower thought. He made a note to get Tizzard to find out. The late Mrs. Martin's touches were also still evident from the fading but still colourful curtains to the hand-made lace doilies under all of the lamps. One dirty cup along with its partner plate in the sink and a cold, stinky half pot of tea on the stove were evidence of Elias Martin's last meal. Maybe evidence in court as well, thought Windflower.

Careful not to disturb anything, he moved quietly through the house. Just one solitary portrait of a young Mr. and Mrs. Martin on their wedding day to break the monotony and silence that enveloped the living room. No television, just a small radio on the mantle for comfort and contact with the outside world.

Windflower wandered through the other rooms checking drawers in the one bedroom that was still being used. A dozen pairs of heavy woolen socks, four clean lumberjack shirts and three pairs of long johns. In the closet, two pairs of blue workman pants and, wrapped in plastic, a clean but old fashioned black suit. For weddings and church on Sunday and now his burial suit, he thought. A pair of black dress shoes to go along with work boots, rubber boots and a pair of hip waders. On the hooks hung two woolen fisherman's caps and a fedora with a red feather for Sunday morning. Nothing unusual here.

He went back to the kitchen which may or may not have been the real scene of the crime. Windflower checked the fridge and the small freezer but didn't touch or move anything in case he would contaminate any possible evidence. Not much in there anyway, just some jams and pickles in the fridge and a five litre bottle of water. In the freezer a couple of what looked like moose steaks and a box of chicken parts.

If Elias Martin had been poisoned the proof would likely be somewhere in here. But where? This was clearly a job for the experts thought Windflower. He called back to the detachment and asked his secretary Betsy Malloy to call the RCMP Forensics Unit in St. John's to get them to send a team out to Grand Bank to check out the house.

"Don't you need the Inspector's authorization for that request?" asked Betsy.

"No," snapped Windflower.

"I was just trying to be helpful," said Betsy.

"Sorry Betsy, just make the call okay."

"Okay Sergeant, but he won't likely be happy," Betsy replied.

"Don't worry Betsy, I'll look after the Inspector," he said although he knew that this wouldn't be easy. As soon as MacIntosh found out about the forensics request he'd have Windflower's ass in Marystown faster than the fog rolled in over the Cape.

Oh well, that gives me about a day and a half to get some real evidence to support the extra expenses I've just approved without authorization, Windflower thought. I can live with that.

As he left Elias Martin's home Sergeant Windflower took one more look around outside as he circled the front of the house with yellow police caution tape to warn the curious away. Nice picket fence freshly limed; a stack of firewood neatly piled by the back door and next winter's supply stacked in the nearby shed. Some rotten lobster traps, balls of fishing twine and a few empty plastic water bottles like the one in the fridge. A nice, safe, clean and quiet house in a small Newfoundland outport. Could the man who lived here really have been intentionally killed? And by whom?

Chapter Six

Windflower's cell phone broke his reverie in a hurry.

"Windflower," he said.

"Hey Sergeant, it's Vinjay. I just got a call from the Minister at the Anglican Church. He wants to know if we can release the body so that they can go ahead with the funeral. It's okay by me. I've got all the tox reports but I wanted to check with you. Is it all right, by?"

"Sounds okay to me," said Windflower. "Did the Minister say when the funeral would be?"

"Friday morning at ten," said the doctor.

"By the way, who's his next of kin?" asked Windflower.

"Elias Martin has a sister in Ontario. As far as I know that's his only living relative although he probably has a bunch of cousins all over the South Coast. I have her number somewhere here in the file, do you want it?"

"Yeah, maybe I'll give her a call."

"It's Georgette Sheridan. She's in Waterloo, Ontario. Here's her phone number."

"Thanks, Doc. I'll talk to you later."

Maybe the sister could tell him something about Elias Martin that would help Windflower start to make sense out of what was going on here. He sure needed help from someone.

As Windflower pulled his cruiser out of the Martin driveway he noticed that the curtains on most of the nearby neighbours' houses were opened just a peek. I bet we got their attention now, he thought.

He started to head back to the office to start the endless paperwork that would accompany an investigation like this and he wanted to make sure he got it right, especially with MacIntosh breathing down his neck. Then his stomach grumbled to remind him that he hadn't eaten anything since a granola bar for breakfast.

A nice bowl of hot soup would do the trick, he thought, and as if automatically the cruiser turned down the laneway that led to the Mug-Up. All heads swiveled towards him as he opened the door and strode to the counter to place his order. "I'll have a bowl of turkey soup and a roll please, Marie," he told the waitress at the cash.

"Coming right up. Why don't you take a seat and I'll bring it over, my ducky." Marie smiled.

"Thanks," mumbled Windflower, his stomach in the café but his head miles away as he thought again about Elias Martin's lonely house and how he ended up dead on the Cape.

As Marie was delivering Windflower's soup, Constable Tizzard burst into the café like a gale-force wind. Tizzard nodded to all the customers and then spotted Windflower in the corner.

"Hi Sarge," breezed Tizzard. "Just poppin in for a cuppa. Cup of tea, Marie, my love," he called out to the harried waitress at the counter.

Windflower had to smile at Tizzard's youthful enthusiasm but wondered if he had the maturity, and more importantly the discretion, to carry out his end of the investigation.

"Come and sit down Tizzard," said Windflower. "Keep your voice down but tell me what you've found out."

"Well the funeral is on Friday morning. I talked to Minister Franklin at the Anglican church."

"Tell me something I don't know," said Windflower.

"Glad you asked, Sarge," said Tizzard. "According to the Minister Elias Martin was a quiet church going regular with few enemies."

"No news there," said Windflower.

"I said few enemies, not none, Sarge," smiled Tizzard.

"Spill the beans, Tizzard, you're trying my patience."

"Well it appears that Elias Martin had a young shipmate during his fishing years; Roger Buffet's son, Jarge, and he was lost at sea during a storm about twenty-five years ago. The long liner they were sailing on hit a reef just outside the harbour and young Jarge was swept overboard. His body was never found."

"So it was an accident at sea?" asked Windflower.

"Well that was Elias Martin's story but Roger Buffet blamed Elias. I guess Jarge was a little slow, if you know what I mean, and Roger had never wanted Elias to let him go out to sea. He's been mad at Elias Martin ever since. Over the years he's been arrested for mischief a number of times, including once when he tried to burn down the Martin house with two cans of gasoline.

Everybody I talked to said that Roger Buffet is still a bitter man over what happened to Jarge."

"But Elias Martin was apparently poisoned, not burnt to death," said Windflower.

"Wait, Sarge, there's more. Roger Buffet wasn't the only one who held a grudge against Elias Martin."

"It also appears that Mr. Martin may have lost a few more friends when he ran over a young girl about two years ago. The girl's name was Ginger Grandy and she was hit by old Elias coming home one foggy night. She was seriously hurt and is still in a wheelchair. The Grandy girl's parents were quite upset about the accident. They moved to St. John's so that they could get her the best of treatment and that's probably a good thing for the old guy. He was pretty shook up about it and never drove a car again after that. He sold his old Dodge truck to Wally Sparks down the road."

"Wow, Elias Martin sure had his share of accidents, didn't he?" commented Windflower.

"Yes, especially in the last couple of years", said Tizzard. "But it gets even better."

Chapter Seven

"Someone else may have wanted Elias Martin dead," said Tizzard.

"After Eileen Martin died Elias apparently tried to rekindle an old flame. Unfortunately for him, her husband didn't think too kindly of that idea."

Both men paused as Marie brought Windflower his soup and Tizzard his mug of hot black tea.

"Are you sure about this, Tizzard?" asked Windflower, sipping on his still hot broth. "Elias Martin must have been in his sixties."

"I guess the furnace was still burning bright under that mountain of snow," said Tizzard. "And my source is impeccable."

"Your cousin, Matilda?" asked Windflower, identifying the chief busybody and gossip trader in Grand Bank.

"Not just Matilda, I confirmed it with the experts down at the wharf," said Tizzard, referring to the morning gathering of old-timers who met each morning to share memories and most importantly all of the latest gossip and local dirt.

"So who is this mystery woman, and who is her husband?" asked Windflower, by now eagerly digging into the soft morsels of turkey and vegetables in his bowl.

"The woman is Marge Brenton and her husband is Harvey. Both Harvey and Elias Martin grew up in Frenchman's Cove and Marge moved there with her family when her father came in as schoolteacher years ago. Elias and Harvey both chased Marge and while Marge apparently favoured Elias, her family thought Brenton was a better match because his family had money and Elias was just a poor fisherman. Elias was pushed out of the way and eventually moved to Grand Bank because he couldn't stand the sight of his beloved in another man's arms."

"Great romance and great gossip," said Windflower. "But is all this enough to get a man killed?"

"Well, Harvey Brenton publicly threatened to kill Elias if he didn't stay away from his wife, and last year there was a report of someone firing shots at Martin's house," said Tizzard. "The investigation couldn't prove that Brenton did it, but he was the prime suspect, and he does have a large collection of guns and ammo."

"Probably just like half the other men on the South Coast," said Windflower. "But given what we have to go on so far it makes sense to follow up. Why don't you go over and interview the Brentons, and if you can, try to talk to them separately? Also, can you see what Roger Buffet is up to these days as well and get me a number for the Grandy's in St. John's? I'll give them a call myself," added Windflower. Tizzard nodded and was getting up to go when Marie dropped by the table again. "Everything okay, m'dears?" she asked.

"Soup's great as usual, Marie," said Windflower.

"Oh, by the way, Sheila left a message for you to call her if you came in, Sergeant," said Marie.

Windflower's cheeked flushed a little and his dark eyes glinted steel at Tizzard who slurped a few more sips of tea and headed out with a smile but wisely without a word.

"Thanks, Marie, I'll call her later," said Windflower.

As Windflower scooped up the last of his savoury soup with his roll he thought pleasantly about Sheila, but soon his mind was refocused on the case at hand. His assignments to Tizzard might be wild goose chases, he thought, but maybe somewhere in all of this there might be a motive. After paying his bill with a dozen pairs of eyes intently following his every move he decided to take a closer look at where the body had been found.

He drove to the Cove and now that the fog had lifted, if briefly, he decided to take a walk up to the Cape and retrace Elias Martin's last steps. Maybe it was the Indian in him, or his inner police instinct, but maybe, just maybe he could find something, anything that would help decipher the code of this unexpected death.

Windflower strode over the rocky beach and followed the well worn path where Elias Martin had spent so many mornings. The wind was brisk but at least the sun was out and it had chased the fog bank back towards the French islands of St. Pierre and Miquelon. He climbed effortlessly over the barrens and onto the steeper inclines where only wild berry bushes and errant sea gulls wandered.

This path had once been the most direct route to Fortune on the other side of the hills and young men and sometimes a few young women would walk this narrow passageway to go to the dance there on Saturday night. These days only a few tourists and a scattering of locals like Elias Martin would make this a part of their daily exercise routine. And nobody would think of walking the ten miles to Fortune any more. Not when they had a pickup truck and a perfectly good paved highway to get there.

He paused at the peak to survey the vast landscape of sea and endless sky. It was a long way from home in Alberta but sometimes the emptiness of this space reminded him of the prairies and foothills of his place of birth. He said a silent prayer for his family and his people who still lived there, and even for the spirit of the newly departed Elias Martin. He didn't know Martin but he did believe that the spirits of the dead sometimes lingered near the place where they died. Maybe that would lead him to something.

He wandered back down the hill along the path and saw the police tape where the body had been discovered. This was a very ordinary location to die, he thought. No trees or bushes surrounded the area and if there was any evidence it would have likely been carried away by now by scavenging gulls or the ever present wind.

Just as he was about to leave for the final descent he noticed it, clinging to a blackberry bush. It was a brown silken scarf, clearly a woman's. The two tourists who found the body had been males and Elias Martin would hardly have worn a lady's scarf with his fisherman's attire. That meant that there had been a woman on the Cape at some time in the recent past. Was she here with Elias Martin or just another tourist or healthy-minded local out for a stroll?

But it was interesting that a lady's scarf had been found so close to where Elias Martin had taken his last steps and final breath. Did that person know anything about his death and could she have possibly had anything to do with it?

Just what I need thought Windflower, more questions. But, he said to himself, carefully placing the scarf into a plastic evidence bag, at least I have one piece of solid evidence.

Chapter Eight

Sergeant Windflower pulled his coat collar up to stave off the cooling wind that was blowing the fog back onto shore from the ocean and creeping back into Grand Bank. It's like the old joke about Newfoundland weather, he thought; if you don't like the weather, don't worry, it will change any minute. He got back into his cruiser and headed towards the detachment.

When he arrived he was surprised to see Inspector MacIntosh's staff car parked in front of the building. Oh, well, he thought, better get this over with. Betsy half smiled, half grimaced as she nodded to him on his way in, her eyes pointing to his office where the Inspector awaited.

"Good afternoon, Inspector," said Windflower. "What can I do for you?"

Inspector MacIntosh was a tall broad man with a graying mustache and a stern Scottish temperament that could easily burst into a flaming outrage at the slightest provocation. It was clear to Windflower from MacIntosh's glare that his pilot light had already been turned on.

"What the hell do you think you're playing at?" he bellowed at Windflower. "Who gave you the authority to call St. John's to order forensics and what in the name of sweet Jesus made you think I wouldn't hear about it?"

Windflower slowly turned and closed his office door, partly to give him time to frame his response but more to save Betsy from hearing his Boss strip his hide. He took a deep breath and started to try and tell this fire breathing dragon his side of the story.

"Well, Inspector, I made the decision to call forensics because I felt that there was more to Elias Martin's death than just a simple stroke or heart attack and if that was the case then the faster we move to gather evidence then the easier it will be to solve this case. We now have a death certificate signed by the chief medical officer stating that a factor in Mr. Martin's death was almost certainly, poisoning, arsenic poisoning, sir. I tried to call you but you were out of town and not expected back for a few days so I took the action I thought was required."

"Arsenic poisoning, my arse," barked MacIntosh. "You've been reading too many murder mysteries, Windflower, but even if this was a suspicious death, the protocol is for you to get permission before accessing any outside resources. I found out about your request via a call from Superintendant MacCauley in St. John's. How stupid do you think that made me look when I didn't have a sweet foggy clue what was going on in my own patch?"

"I'm sorry sir," said Windflower, but MacIntosh stopped him short.

"You'll be sorry all right," said the Inspector. "I'm putting you on official notice of potential discipline for ignoring the chain of command and if this turns out to be a wild goose chase, then you can kiss those stripes goodbye. I will not have any renegade investigations on my watch. Is that clear Windflower?"

"Yes, sir," said Windflower, knowing the threat to be real and well within MacIntosh's authority.

"Now give me the story from the very beginning and I expect to have a full written report by e-mail tonight," said MacIntosh. He seemed happier to have restored his complete superiority over this independent minded Sergeant.

Thirty minutes later Windflower had completed his verbal report as the Superintendant sat and listened.

"So you have a couple of decades old enemies and a lady's scarf to go on so far," chuckled MacIntosh. "Not much to go to court with yet."

"Not yet, sir, but our investigation is just beginning," said Windflower.

"It may be over faster than you think," said MacIntosh. "I'll let you have the forensics team and three days to come up with something more concrete. After that I'll make the decision about where we go next. If anything develops and I mean anything, I want to be the first to know. If I hear about it from someone else I'll have your balls for bookends."

"One more thing Windflower. Be careful about who you stir up in this investigation. This is a small community that guards its secrets and its own very closely. They don't take lightly to outsiders poking their noses into their private affairs. You may move on in a few years, sooner if you keep pissing me off, but some of us plan to be here for a long time."

Windflower bristled at the implied threat in the Inspector's last comment but decided to keep his powder dry, at least for now.

"We will follow all correct protocol in this investigation, sir," he replied.

"Do that, Sergeant, just be careful about whose toes you step on."

With that MacIntosh breezed out of the office and peeled gravel as he left the parking lot, leaving Windflower feeling like a horse that had been ridden hard and put away wet.
His head ached and his emotions ranged from anger to excitement. Macintosh had given him the green light to proceed and three days to make some headway. It was clear to

Windflower that he already had. Somebody had gotten to his Inspector. Otherwise why would he have given him the warning about stepping on the wrong toes? That's good, thought Windflower. Maybe by stirring things up it would finally lead him closer to the truth about the dead man on the Cape.

Chapter Nine

A small dram of dark rum, a hot cup of tea, and a half hour soaking in his tub made Windflower feel sleepy but normal again. Shoot, he thought, I forgot to call Sheila back.

He thought about Sheila Hillier as he fumbled through his address book looking for her phone number. Something in her easy smile, her long red hair and her rollicking laughter brought him a little joy, even on his darkest days. That and her comfortable sensuality and even longer legs brought another warm sensation.

They had shared a few quiet and memorable evenings together over a bottle of wine and a well cooked meal but something in both of them kept them from moving to the next level of a relationship. Maybe he was really too much of an outsider for her to consider, or maybe it was him that he just didn't see getting serious about a woman when he might only be here for another year or so. He had joined the Mounties for a job and now realized he had married a career.

Somehow they both decided to just accept what they had, at least for now. A quiet comfort and a good friend to talk to. A good friend, thought Windflower as Sheila answered the phone, that's what I really need right now.

"Evening, Sheila, how are you?"

"Hi Winston, I'm fine thank you very much. I was hoping to reach you earlier to invite you over for supper. My nephew, Jabe, brought me a brace of rabbits and I thought you might like some rabbit stew. But I guess it's probably too late now," she said sounding a little disappointed.

"That is too bad," said Windflower. "I love rabbit stew. Sorry I didn't get back to you earlier but I've had a hell of a day."

"I guess you're working on that Martin case," said Sheila. "You don't have to tell me anything if you don't want to, but you've sure created some conversation at the Mug-Up."

"Is that so?" Windflower laughed in return.

"Yes indeed," said Sheila. "If you'd like a little warmed over stew and a piece of partridge berry crumble I can fill you in on the latest gossip."

"Well, Mrs. Hillier, that's the best offer I've had all day. I don't know if the gossip will be worth it, but your home-cooking surely will."

"Always the charmer Sergeant Windflower. See you soon."

Windflower smiled to himself in the mirror as he shaved and put on his civvies. Maybe a little aftershave cologne as well he thought. You never know what can happen.

He pulled on his windbreaker and stuffed his hands in his pockets as he strolled from his small bungalow near the new supermarket to Sheila's house in the centre of town. He loved the fact that you could walk just about everywhere in Grand Bank, although most locals drove their heavy duty pickup trucks almost all the time. The short walk gave him time to think and to wake up a little from his bath time reverie.

Before he knew it he was at Sheila's back door. That was another thing he liked about this small community. No one used the front door unless it was to greet the clergy on their yearly home visits. Friends and neighbours knew to just come around the back and walk right into the kitchen.

Windflower could smell the rabbit stew before he saw Sheila, stirring the pot and singing quietly to herself. "Evening Sheila," he called out as he took off his boots and hung his coat up on the pegs near the door.

"Sit down, Winston, and take a load off the world," she called back.

Windflower sat at the kitchen table as she placed a large bowl of fragrant stew topped with a thin slightly browned pastry crust in front of him. "Dig in," she said. As Windflower savoured the succulent pieces of stewed rabbit and vegetables she offered him a glass of wine and sat with hers to join him.

"This is fabulous, Sheila," he said. "Aren't you having any?"

"I had a taste earlier," Sheila said. "You kind of lose your appetite when you're cooking for people all day. But I love to see a man eat. Sometimes I think that's what I miss most about not having Bart around. Oh, and the other stuff too," she laughed.

"You are certainly a fine cook, Ms. Hillier, but I'm not going to touch that other comment with a ten foot pole," he laughed back. That was part of their usual friendly banter. It was pleasant and human. It didn't avoid the hard stuff but still allowed them to have a little fun together.

As he soaked up the last of his stew with a thick piece of home-made bread he sighed and said "Mrs. Hillier I think that's the best rabbit stew I've ever had."

"Thank you for the compliment Sergeant. I presume you are hoping for a return engagement."

"That would be great," he replied. "But actually I was hoping that I could return the favour by taking you out for dinner on the weekend. We could take the RCMP launch over to St. Pierre and try out one of the new bistros everybody is talking about. The skipper on the boat is an old buddy of mine and he's offered to take me over and back."

Sheila blushed deeply despite herself and said "That sounds nice Winston, but won't it get the tongues wagging around here?"

"Speaking of tongues wagging, why don't you fill me in on the latest news from the Mug-Up?"

"I'll put the kettle on," Sheila said. "This may take a while."

Chapter Ten

Sheila brought the tray with two china cups and a beautiful cozy-covered tea pot into the living room and laid it on the coffee table. She poured a cup for Windflower and one for herself.

"So what are the local experts saying about the Martin case?" asked Windflower.

"Well you've certainly got them in an uproar," said Sheila. "Most of them can't believe that anyone would really hurt old Elias, but he really was a weird stick."

"Did you know him?" asked Windflower.

"Just enough to nod to him at church on Sunday but I can remember overhearing my Dad talk to Mom about him a few times." Both of Sheila's parents had passed on in the past few years, the victims of living in a harsh climate with little real medical attention until recently.

"When his wife Eileen was alive he seemed to be doing okay but after her death he seemed to crumble a bit," she said.

"I guess that's not unusual," said Windflower. "She was probably his anchor in life. They didn't have any children, did they?"

"No, it was just the two of them. Eileen still has a couple of brothers living in Frenchman's Cove and Elias has a sister in Ontario."

"Georgette isn't it?" asked Windflower.

"Yes that's her. She came down to visit a few times after Eileen's death and I think she is the only one who still called him up to check in on him. Everyone else thought he went a little weird. I actually found him a little pathetic," said Sheila.

"Pathetic? In what way?" asked Windflower.

"According to the folks around here, especially the experts on the wharf, they believe he went balmy after his wife died. There was that big stink over the Buffet kid's drowning on his boat and many people felt that Elias should never have allowed young Jarge on his boat, particularly Roger Buffet."

"Wasn't it an accident?" asked Windflower.

"I guess so," said Sheila "but none of the other fisherman went out on the day Jarge drowned because of a storm that was brewing off the coast, and the kid wasn't all there if you know what I mean. His father had driven him off his boat and in spite he signed up with Skipper Martin who needed help and probably thought he was doing the young fella a favour."

"Roger Buffet was beside himself, first with Elias Martin defying his orders to his son and then taking unnecessary risks that led to his drowning. He warned Elias Martin about taking the boy out and after his death threatened to kill him right on the wharf in front of everybody."

"Do you think he meant it?" asked Windflower.

"When he had enough rum in him he certainly talked like he was serious," said Sheila. "He was hauled into court a few years back for trying to burn down the Martin house."

"I guess that was pretty serious," said Windflower, thinking that both grief and revenge were great motives.

"It was, except that Roger Buffet spent three days telling everybody in town what he was planning to do and then two more days getting enough drunk courage to carry it out. By the time he got to the Martin house with two jerry cans of gasoline your fellow Mounties were waiting for him before he could light the fuse. Check your files, Sergeant."

"Oh, I've got Tizzard working on that angle. Besides I'd much rather deal with a pretty informant like you, Sheila."

"You are a charmer, Sergeant, but you haven't even given me a crumb of information yet. The word at the café is that Elias Martin was poisoned? Is that true?"

"That is a possibility that we're not ruling out, but until the forensics people get here we won't know for sure. At this point we're treating the death as suspicious but until we get some more evidence we can't really be sure."

As much as Windflower liked and admired Sheila he didn't want to broadcast his suspicion of arsenic poisoning. He didn't want that out in the public domain until there was some way to link a possible suspect with the certain death. The fewer people who knew about the potential cause of death, the better. If there was a murderer in the community he didn't want them to start covering up their tracks even more. He decided to switch the subject to more comfortable ground, at least for him.

"What about the situation with the Grandy girl?" he asked. "That must have had quite an impact on both old Elias and the community as well".

"Yes," said Sheila, "Ginger Grandy was such a nice young girl and both her family and Elias were pretty broken up about that. Her father, Ches, was a good friend of Bart's so we saw them a lot when Bart was around." For a moment Sheila's eyes glazed over but she blinked quickly and continued, "Ches and his wife were devastated. Ginger was their only child."

"Were the Grandys angry at Elias Martin?" asked Windflower.

"Ches was out of his mind for a few weeks but then the focus was on getting Ginger back to health. I haven't heard from them in over a year since they went to St. John's but I get news from some of the locals who travel back and forth that she is still in rehabilitation. They're still hoping she can walk again. My heart goes out to them," said Sheila.

"What about Elias after this happened?" asked Windflower. "Did he go over to the Grandy's to apologize?"

"I guess he tried to," said Sheila "but Ches Grandy kicked him out of his house and told him to go to hell and never come back. We all learned never to raise Elias Martin's name in that household again."

"That's very interesting, how so many bad things seemed to happen to one old man, don't you think?" asked Windflower. Sheila just looked at him quietly but lost in her own thoughts, did not respond.

"I did find one interesting thing on the Cape today when I went up for a stroll around," said Windflower. "A lady's silk scarf."

"That is interesting," said Sheila. "Lots of women wear scarves to church but there aren't too many who take the walk up to the Cape these days. It's been years since I've been there myself. Those ladies who do walk usually power walk around town rather than heading up into the hills. Who do you think the scarf belongs to?"

"I have no idea," said Windflower. "And Inspector MacIntosh didn't think much of my only piece of evidence either."

"MacIntosh is a bit of a blowhard, isn't he?" asked Sheila.

Windflower wondered what the Inspector had done to get under the friendly café owner's skin but decided to be more diplomatic. "He may be, but he's just doing his job. I have another couple of days to come up with something more substantial or he'll take over the case himself. Back to the late Mr. Martin, did he have any other people who didn't like him?" asked Windflower.

"Elias Martin was a crooked old man who didn't seem to care who liked him or not," said Sheila. "But in terms of enemies, Harvey Brenton was probably at the top of the list."

"That name has come up already. What can you tell me about him?"

"There's lot to tell about Harvey Brenton," she said, pausing for a moment. "He's not a man that you want to mess with in this community or anywhere else on the Southeast Coast. If we are going to talk about Harvey Brenton I'd better put another pot of tea on," said Sheila.

Windflower was a little surprised, both by Sheila's sudden seriousness and by the fact that she was the second person that day to warn him to be careful with this investigation. There was certainly a lot more he wanted to know about Harvey Brenton and if he was dangerous enough to be responsible for murder.

Chapter Eleven

Windflower followed Sheila back to the kitchen and watched as she filled the kettle and plugged it in. "Tizzard has already given me the gossip overview on that situation. It appears that Martin and Brenton go back a long ways as rivals," he said.

"That's the story," said Sheila "and after Eileen Martin died apparently Elias tried for a second chance."

"I guess Mr. Brenton wasn't too impressed," said Windflower.

"No, and Elias Martin picked the wrong man to rile up," said Sheila. "Harvey Brenton is a very well connected man all over the South Coast. He is also known to have a very mean streak for anyone who crosses him in business, politics, or his personal life. He is not a person that you want to be on the wrong side of, if you want to have a successful police career or even a successful coffee shop."

Windflower sensed that there was another story underneath Sheila's comments but unless she wanted to divulge the details he didn't want to appear too nosy.

"I'm just doing my job, Ma'am," he said, hoping to get the conversation back on a lighter level.

Sheila smiled. "You're a good man, Winston. Just remember that there are always secrets in a small community that someone wants to protect."

That was his second warning about secrets in one day too, thought Windflower. Either I'm starting to get closer to the truth or deeper into hot water.

"Thanks for the advice, Sheila, and of course the fine rabbit stew," he said.

"I almost forgot about dessert," said Sheila as she got up to turn off the boiling water. "My partridgeberry crumble is just cooling in the fridge."

"I can't eat another bite," protested Windflower "and I have to head back home soon."

"I'll wrap up a piece for you to take with you," she insisted. This time Windflower smiled. This is a nice woman, he thought. A man could get used to this treatment.

Sheila met him at the back door with his dessert in a cute little cake tin and a twinkle in her eyes.

"Thank you for a lovely evening Sheila," he said. "The food and the company were as wonderful as ever."

"You're very welcome, Winston," she replied. "Anytime."

Windflower took the tin from her hands and, not sure what to do, gave her a hug goodbye. Friendly, but not too much, he thought, but he was sure she was pulling him closer in response. He kissed her on the forehead.

"Goodnight Sheila, don't forget about Saturday night."

"It's a date," she said.

I think it is, thought Windflower as he started his walk back through town. He felt warm and a little tingly all over despite the fog and the Northeast wind that had started to kick up a bit. Rain tomorrow, his Indian bones told him.

By the time he got home he was tired and ready for bed. Just as he started to let himself relax he remembered that he still had to send Inspector MacIntosh his report.

He powered up his computer and began writing up what he had so far. It wasn't much so he took a few minutes longer to embellish it before he sent it off. He knew he wasn't going to fool MacIntosh but given the warnings he'd had today he wanted to make sure he covered all his bases.

Finally, he was done, and as he remembered his final hug with Sheila he felt a little warm and maybe a bit more of that tingly stuff too. Before he had time to further analyze these feelings Sergeant Winston Windflower was fast asleep.

Chapter Twelve

As Windflower was falling into dreamland his young Constable was just getting home. He'd been off duty for a while and had dropped in to the local lounge to have a beer and a game of darts with his buddies on the way home. That had been the most relaxing portion of his day. The other parts had been both a little exciting and a little intense.

He had followed up by interviewing more of the neighbours and then went to see Roger Buffet. But it was too late in the day to get any sense out of Mr. Buffet. By the time he had gotten to his house Buffet had been passed out for an hour or so, according to his wife, and judging by her nonchalant demeanor, Tizzard assumed that this might be a daily occurrence. He decided to head back over in the morning and maybe he should ask his Sergeant to come along.

That's because his second interaction with witnesses had been of the most unpleasant sort. Tizzard had arrived at Harvey and Marge Brenton's large two-story home overlooking the water. Pretty nice, thought Tizzard, easily the most extensive property in the area, with its own private dock and a nice sized yacht tied up alongside what appeared to be a very fast-looking speedboat. "I bet those toys cost a pretty penny and probably a few runs made over to St. Pierre, along the smuggler's route too," thought Tizzard.

Tizzard rapped on the large door knocker and was greeted by what was obviously the housekeeper. "Can I help youse?" she asked.

"I'd like to see Mr. or Mrs. Brenton," answered Tizzard.

"If you'd like to wait here I'll tell the missus," said the housekeeper, who then went off into the back rooms leaving Tizzard free to have a look around at the high ceilings and elaborate woodworked interior of the Brenton home. He noticed a picture, an etching, and a really good one, he thought. He looked for the signature and saw that it was by David Blackwood, one of Newfoundland's most famous artists. Tizzard wasn't a true aficionado of art, but he knew the real thing when he saw it.

"I have a few more Blackwoods in the living room, if you want to follow me, Constable", said an elegant but older lady that Tizzard knew must be the "missus".

"Thank you, Mrs. Brenton. I'm Constable Edward Tizzard," said the young RCMP officer.

"You can call me Marge and unless I'm mistaken you're probably better known as Eddie," said Mrs. Brenton. "What can I do for you, Constable?"

Tizzard noted as he followed behind her that Mrs. Brenton, Marge, was still a good looking woman, well dressed and 'done up to the nines', as his Mother would say, even at this time of day.

When they reached the living room he noticed at least two more Blackwoods and two Pratts (a Mary and a Christopher) as well. His first year class in Newfoundland art was finally paying off.

"I really like your pictures, Mrs. Brenton, I mean Marge," he stammered.

"One of my passions, or my weaknesses, my children like to say," said the older lady. "But you didn't come here to admire my artwork, did you Constable?"

"No ma'am," said Tizzard. "I'm here to talk to you about the late Elias Martin."

"I guessed as much," Marge Brenton said. "Sit down, Eddie and I'll get Beulah to get us some tea." She rang a small silver bell on a nearby glass coffee table and folded her hands in her lap. "This is very hard for me to talk about. I feel like I've lost one of my best friends. It is such a shame. He didn't deserve this."

"Deserve what?" asked Tizzard.

Just then a cool wind rushed into the room followed closely by what Tizzard knew had to be Harvey Brenton. This new arrival was soon toe to toe with the RCMP Constable, who luckily was about a foot and a half taller.

"What the hell are you doing in my house?" bellowed Mr. Brenton as he reached up to jab his finger into Tizzard's chest.

Tizzard stepped back momentarily and then, resuming control, moved Harvey Brenton's hand to one side and simply said "Don't touch me again, Mr. Brenton. I'm here to ask you and your wife some questions about Elias Martin, sir. And we can do it here or at the detachment," he said calmly but sternly. "If you have any questions you can talk to Sergeant Windflower. He's in charge of the investigation."

"Don't worry. I'll be talking to your Sergeant," said Harvey Brenton. "He may be in charge now, but he may not be long. Now get the hell out of my house."

Tizzard gathered up his hat and notebook, said goodbye to Mrs. Brenton and left as slowly as his anxiety would allow.

Outside he breathed a short sigh of relief and then decided that he would take a little break to slow down his heartbeat. He was grateful that he didn't over react in this tense situation but he had to admit that it had been a long time since he had felt such intense anger so close up. If he hadn't been well-trained as an RCMP officer, he might have even admitted to being a little afraid.

Chapter Thirteen

Sergeant Windflower woke to the blaring alarm of the country music station on his radio. It wasn't that he was a big country western fan. It was just the only music that could raise him enough to want to turn it off. He stared at the glowing red light on the radio. 6:45 it blinked back.

Windflower got up out of bed and went to the kitchen to put on his coffee and gazed out his back window into an impenetrable blanket of fog, and as he had predicted a steady rain. While he waited for his coffee he gathered up his medicine pouch and smudge bowl and pulled his parka on over his pajamas. It was part of Windflower's morning routine to try and connect with his native spirituality and it was one of the few things that kept him grounded and in touch with who he really was.

He stepped out into the damp darkness of the morning, filled his bowl with the combination of sage and sweet grass that his Elder had given him before he left Pink Lake. He didn't turn on any lights. He wasn't sure what the neighbours would think of their crazy Indian policeman squatting in the darkness burning some wacky tobaccy and he didn't want to draw any more attention to himself than already existed.

He watched as the smoke from the smudge bowl started to rise and slowly passed it over himself with the eagle feather that had once belonged to his grandfather, a respected warrior and leader of his nation. He let the taste and aroma of the smudge enter into his pores and deeper inside of his spirit. He prayed for his family, his ancestors, and mostly for himself. To give him wisdom and courage to do the right thing. He would probably need that today in his work.

After the smoke had dissipated he went back inside and had a cup of coffee while he shaved. He put an egg on to boil and stepped into the shower. The hot water was a welcome relief from the chills of the morning air and as the warm spikes hit his body he really began to wake up, and to start thinking about his day. By the time he'd finished his hard-boiled egg was done and along with a slice of toast and an overripe banana made Windflower's favourite breakfast.

As he ate he jotted down his list of things to do for the day. He needed to stop into the detachment to check on what else had been happening besides his ever-consuming Martin investigation, he needed a report from Tizzard on his interviews, he had to meet up with the forensic guys who were coming in from St. John's, and, he remembered, I have to call Elias Martin's sister in Ontario. List and breakfast completed, he cleaned up his dishes, turned off the coffee pot, and headed over to the RCMP detachment to get to work.

When he arrived Betsy was already hard at work making photocopies in the back. "Morning, Betsy", he called out as he headed into his office. "Can you come see me when you get a chance?"

He poured himself a cup of coffee and reviewed the neat stack of pink message slips on his desk. Calls from local organizations looking for a police officer to attend events, one from the Mayor (probably asking what the RCMP are doing about the kids drinking under the wharf), and one from Inspector MacIntosh. No surprise there. Once the Inspector got a whiff of something in his region he was not one to relax and let things unfold. He wanted action, but most importantly he wanted information.

"Good morning Sergeant," said Betsy, stepping into his office. "I see you've got your messages.

"Yes. Thanks, Betsy. Can you return these messages from the groups that want an officer for show and tell and tell them we'd be happy to do it and then run through the schedule and assign an officer? I'll call the Mayor first thing."

"Inspector MacIntosh also called, did you notice that sir?" asked Betsy.

"Yeah, I saw that one. I'll call him this morning as well," said Windflower. "Have we heard from the forensic guys?

"Yes," said Betsy, "a Staff Sergeant Genges called late yesterday. They are cleaning up a crime scene in St. John's and will try and be here by lunch time."

"Great. As soon as they get here will you call me and I'll come meet them," said Windflower. "So what else has been going on around here in the last few days?"

Betsy pulled open the report file and said "Mostly just the usual. A few complaints about loud music at that new apartment building out by Sobeys, a couple of fender benders, and a fight at Tuckers Lounge about 2 a.m. last night. There was an accident early this morning between a car and a moose. It looks like the moose got the worst of it for a change. Other than that, not too much really."

"Who's on duty roster this week?" asked Windflower.

"Lewis and Fortier," said Betsy. "Willis is on training and should be back late tonight and Lapierre is off sick, again."

Windflower could hear the irritation in her voice as she spoke about the last officer. Betsy was a true believer in the calling of the RCMP, and didn't like slackers, which she apparently thought Lapierre to be. Even though she was a civilian member, she took her work seriously and expected everyone else to do the same.

"Let Lapierre know that I want to see him when he gets back," said Windflower.

Betsy smiled and said "I'll make a note of that". Her mission complete she left the office and Windflower could hear her singing to herself at the photocopier.

At least one person is happy with me, he thought. Now, let's try the Inspector. He rang the Marystown office and got Inspector MacIntosh's secretary. The Inspector was at meetings all morning so a relieved Windflower left a message and hung up.

Next up, the Mayor. Windflower dialed into the Mayor's office and within seconds was talking to, or rather listening to Francis Tibbo's much-repeated diatribe against the young people of today and their neglectful parents. Windflower listened quietly until a pause in the action and then said "Well we do have regular patrols and if that doesn't work then maybe we can try picking a few of them up and bringing them home to the parents?"

Tibbo paused a little and said "Perhaps you should do that, Sergeant." But then thinking of his own political scalp and the angry parents that would end up at his door he added, "But I'm not telling you how to do your police work." Satisfied that he had made his point and would not be held responsible for the fallout, the Mayor said goodbye.

Windflower smiled as he replaced the receiver. Oh the joys of local law enforcement. Maybe we will pick up a few of those underage drinkers, he thought. Maybe even the Mayor's nephew who's down there every Friday night. Just as Windflower was formulating his plan to combat youth mischief in Grand Bank, Constable Tizzard poked his head into his office.

"Morning Sarge," he said. "Got a few minutes for me?"

"Sure thing, Tizzard. What have you got?" asked Windflower.

"Well I'm not sure what it all means but it seems not everybody is happy with our investigation, sir," he said.

"Tell me about it," said Windflower. "MacIntosh is already breathing down my neck. Start from the beginning and tell me about everyone you talked to."

Chapter Fourteen

"I guess I didn't get as far as I'd hoped with my interviews," said Tizzard. "Roger Buffet has been hitting the juice pretty good these days and I thought you and I could see him early this morning if you have no other plans. Better to talk to him hung over than drunk. Also I expect you'll hear from Harvey Brenton. He wasn't too happy with my visit to his home yesterday."

"Is that right?" asked Windflower. "I was kinda looking forward to talking to Mr. Brenton myself. I hear he's a regular Prince Charming."

"Harvey Brenton is one of the angriest men I have ever met," stated Tizzard. "I can see why some people feel intimidated by him."

"I imagine I'll be talking to Mr. Brenton later today," said Windflower. "Anything from the neighbours?"

"Not much," said Tizzard. "According to them Elias Martin had always been a bit of a loner and only had a few visitors. Although one of the neighbours said she thought she saw a woman coming out of the house a few times."

"Did they recognize her?" asked Windflower.

"No," said Tizzard. "She wasn't a local and the person who saw her said she was always bundled up, with a scarf covering her head. They said she was middle aged and nicely dressed."

"Did they say the last time they saw this woman?" asked Windflower.

"About a week ago," said Tizzard, consulting his notes again.

Windflower didn't say anything but immediately thought about the scarf that he had placed in the bottom drawer of his desk. He decided not to tell Tizzard about the scarf just yet. He didn't want his Constable jumping to conclusions.

But Tizzard was already leaping. "It might be Marge Brenton, Sarge," he blurted out.

"Yes it might be," said Windflower. "But let's not get too far ahead of ourselves. Good police work requires evidence and not conjecture, (thinking to himself that he sounded too much like Inspector Macintosh) "Anything else?"

"Not much really," said Tizzard, clearly disappointed that his Sergeant didn't share his enthusiasm. "Elias Martin kept to himself, went to church on Sunday, and did his regular walks up to the Cape, sometimes lugging a jug to fill up at the spring on the hill. Other than that a pretty ordinary guy. Retired and waiting to die was how one person put it, especially after the death of his wife."

"Oh, and I've got a phone number for Ches Grandy in St. John's. Here it is," said Tizzard as he handed a slip of paper to Windflower.

"Good work, Constable," said Windflower.

"Thanks Boss," said Tizzard, both pleased and surprised by his Sergeant's response. "What do you want me to do today?"

"Talk to Betsy and see if you can help her out with anything," said Windflower. "We're down a couple of men and I'm sure she could use your assistance." Then seeing Tizzard's disappointment with desk duty he added "And after I get a coffee we can visit Roger Buffet. Later you can come with me to the Martin house when the forensic guys get here."

Tizzard's eyes brightened at the last piece of information. "Sure thing, Sarge," he said and headed out to see the receptionist.

Windflower still didn't know where this investigation was going but some of the pieces were starting to make sense.

Chapter Fifteen

Well, at least we've got a few more leads to follow up thought Windflower. Although he had his doubts about Roger Buffet. That situation should become clearer when they talked to him. And if the Grandys were in St. John's, then how could they be involved? Still more questions than answers, he thought.

Windflower also thought about Tizzard and really meant what he said when he complimented the young constable. Eddie Tizzard reminded Windflower of his early days as a green recruit, eager to show that he had what it took to be a real police officer. At 26, Tizzard was just a year out of basic training at the police academy in Regina and managed to snare an assignment back to his hometown on his first try.

Normally RCMP constables had to serve at least two tours outside their own region before being allowed anywhere near their home. It was designed to give the recruits a chance to learn, and usually screw up, in front of strangers rather than their own people. But Tizzard had been sent to Grand Bank because, quite frankly, no one from the outside seemed to be able to last longer than a year on this rotation. Tizzard hoped to break that pattern and so did Windflower.

At 24, Windflower had already been a police officer with the tribal police in Pink Lake for four years and the last thing he wanted after RCMP graduation was to be assigned anywhere near back home. He had had his fill of domestic disputes fueled by alcohol, children basically abandoned by their parents once they got drunk, and most of all the suicides. He had been the arriving officer on four of them in his first year alone. Teenagers who didn't see any hope or any future in an isolated community racked by poverty and addiction.

Windflower was happy to be assigned to highway traffic patrol in Courtney in the Comox Valley in British Columbia. Sure, there were some terrible accidents, but they were accidents, not the seemingly inevitable destruction that was happening in Pink Lake.

He liked catching speeders too. He'd find the perfect hideout just beyond a bend and wait as the racing cars sped past him and then desperately tried to brake to avoid the radar. But it was always too late. He'd caught another fly in his spider's web. It reminded him a little of hunting. You don't have to go looking for a deer. You just wait for them to come to you.

After Courtney he got transferred twice more. First he went to Winnipeg working with the anti-gang squad that was trying to break the hold that the Indian gangs had on the drug and prostitution business. Then to Halifax where he earned his Sergeant's stripes on assignment at the airport.

Most of the work there was routine, boring, security detail but he had managed to get hooked up with the customs detail. His team had managed to crack the largest cocaine smuggling operation in the region and as a result everyone, including Windflower, got an opportunity to move up in the system.

Now at 32, Winston Windflower felt like a veteran and he was, at least compared to the other officers in Grand Bank. It was up to him to lead on whatever crossed the door in this detachment. Today that meant the Elias Martin case. So, back to work, he thought.

He glanced at his watch. 10:30 it read. That's nine o'clock in Ontario, not too early to call Georgette Sheridan in Waterloo. He dialed the number in his notebook and after a few rings a woman with a noticeable Newfoundland accent answered.

"Can I speak to Mrs. Georgette Sheridan, please?" he asked.

"That's me," said the woman. "Who is calling, please?"

"It's Sergeant Winston Windflower of the Royal Canadian Mounted Police in Grand Bank, Ma'am," he replied. "I'm calling to ask you a few questions about your late brother, Elias Martin."

"Questions?" asked Mrs. Sheridan sounding more than a little perplexed. "I thought my brother died from a heart attack. Do you think something else happened?"

"We don't yet, Mrs. Sheridan," said Windflower. "Right now there are some signs that it might be more than just a heart attack and until we can find out for sure we are treating your brother's death as suspicious. I was wondering if you could tell me a little more about your brother to assist with our investigation."

"Suspicious? What does that mean Sergeant Windflower?" Now the woman on the other end was clearly confused.

"It's Windflower, Ma'am," he said. "Our medical examiner found high levels of a toxic substance in Mr. Martin's body when he performed the autopsy. We don't know how it got there. It is possible that he was poisoned. That's why we're treating his death as suspicious. We've got a forensics team coming in from St. John's to do further tests and we're hoping we'll be able to know more about this situation after that."

"Poisoned? Do you mean to say that Elias was poisoned?" asked the woman on the phone, now seeming more shocked than anything.

"We're really not sure yet how the poison got into Mr. Martin's system," said Windflower. "But we do believe it was a factor in his death."

"Oh, my God," said Mrs. Sheridan. "Elias was a bit of a queer stick, especially after he lost Eileen, but nobody deserves to die like that!!"

"I agree, Mrs. Sheridan, and I apologize for not extending my personal sympathies earlier. A death in the family is always hard," said Windflower, hoping to get the conversation to a place where he could get some information instead of giving it out. "He was your only sibling I understand?" he gently prodded.

Georgette Sheridan, sounding a little more composed now after the RCMP officer's latest intervention, said softly "Yes, he was the last person in my immediate family. I have my own family of course, two sons and a daughter and four grandchildren. But to lose Elias so suddenly was an awful shock."

"It must have been," said Windflower. "When was the last time you saw your brother?"

"I was in Grand Bank a couple of years back but Elias wasn't very good company and I felt like he wanted to get rid of me so that he could be alone. I had planned to stay two weeks but after the first I just packed up and went to stay with my cousin in Mount Pearl. I had enjoyed going to visit Elias when Eileen was alive. We had some great times together."

After a pause that Windflower allowed to continue she went on, "Elias just went downhill after Eileen died. He withdrew from the few friends that he had and shut himself up in his house. He even got rid of his TV and as far as I know the only thing he enjoyed was going for walks and reading, He liked the subscription to the Readers Digest that I sent him every year for Christmas. I used to phone him every couple of weeks after Eileen died just to check in but it was mostly me talking, so after a while I stopped calling, except for Christmas and his birthday."

"Did he have any friends left at all, anybody that he might have confided in?" asked Windflower.

"Elias had a falling out with most of the other old-timers over the death of the Buffet boy and he didn't care much for the young crowd," said Mrs. Sheridan. "He was also pretty broken-up about the accident and as far as I know he stayed home alone most of the time. The only person he ever mentioned to me was Marge Brenton. Apparently she came by to see him every so often to bring him some jam and a loaf of home-made bread."

So Tizzard was right, thought Windflower. Marge Brenton was Elias Martin's mystery guest woman.

Chapter Sixteen

"Marge Brenton," said Windflower. "I understand that her and your brother knew each other from the early days."

"Yes," laughed Georgette Sheridan, her mood finally lightening a little. "I'm a few years younger than Elias but I can remember how crushed he was when she dumped him for Harvey Brenton. He moped around the house for a few months like a sick dog until he finally moved to Grand Bank to work on Skipper Forsey's long liner."

"How well do you know the Brentons?" asked Windflower, deliberately avoiding referring to Harvey Brenton in particular.

"Marge Brenton was always a sweetheart," said the woman. "I knew her when she was Marge Abbott and her father was the principal of the school. Sometimes she would help out in class. And she was quite a beauty in those days too. She had travelled all over with her parents and knew all about make-up and the latest styles. All of the younger girls looked up to her and all of the boys were crazy about her, including my Elias."

"What about Harvey Brenton?" asked Windflower, deciding to finally get to the question he was most curious about.

"Harvey Brenton was a mean spoiled brat," said Mrs. Sheridan. "His family owned the general store and just about everything else in Frenchman's Cove and Harvey thought he was better than everybody else because of it. He was the kind of child who would steal your cat and torture it, just for a laugh, and because he could get away with anything he wanted."

"He had his own car when the rest of us were lucky to have shoes," she continued. "He was an obnoxious young man who only got worse as he got older. Even Marge couldn't get him to change his ways and I always thought she just stayed with him because of their children."

"Is that all, Sergeant? My son is coming to pick me up soon to drive me to the airport so that I can get to Grand Bank for the funeral tomorrow."

"Just one more question, Mrs. Sheridan, if you don't mind," said Windflower. "Was your brother in good health? Did he have any medical conditions?"

"Elias was always as healthy as a horse," said the woman on the end of the line. "But in the last year he started to complain about headaches and stomach pains the few times I talked to him. I told him to see the doctor but he was a stubborn old coot and I don't think he ever went. I guess the other thing is that he was often confused about things. I just thought it was about getting older."

"Thanks very much, Mrs. Sheridan, you have been very helpful. I am sorry that I had to intrude on your grief. I'll see you at the funeral tomorrow and as soon as I have any more information I'll pass it on to you," said Windflower."

"Goodbye, Sergeant," said Mrs. Sheridan and she hung up.

Well, a bit more information, thought Windflower and confirmation of a few things more. Marge Brenton was clearly the woman that the neighbours had seen visiting Elias Martin and Harvey Brenton's ill reputation went a long ways back. The Brentons were becoming the most interesting people in this investigation but as for proof of any wrongdoing, illegal or immoral, his evidence was scarce and none.

Mrs. Sheridan's last answer about Elias Martin's health was interesting and Windflower made a note to ask Doc Sanjay about symptoms of arsenic poisoning when he saw him again. While he scribbled the note Windflower's stomach grumble told him it was time for some toast and tea but before he headed out he called Tizzard into his office.

"Yes, Sarge," said Tizzard, happy to at least be temporarily removed from his paperwork assignment with Betsy.

"Well it appears that you were right," said Windflower. "Georgette Sheridan confirms that Marge Brenton was a sometimes visitor to Elias Martin's house. But let's not read too much into it yet."

Tizzard beamed at the news that he had been right. "Doesn't that tie her into Elias Martin sometime close to when he died?"

"It may mean that she visited him but it doesn't necessarily mean that she had anything to do with his death, Constable," said Windflower. "But I'd sure like to hear what she has to say. I am going to try and talk to her later today."

"What about her husband?" asked Tizzard. "Based on his reaction to me yesterday he surely won't be happy if you start talking to his wife."

"Leave Harvey Brenton to me," said Windflower. "I think Mr. Brenton and I will be having our own chat very soon. I want you to do another thing before the forensics team gets here. Can you find out if Elias Martin had a cleaning lady and if she knows anything that might be interesting?"

"Sure," said Tizzard. "I'll talk to Mavis Emberly. She appears to be the number one scout in the neighbourhood."

"Okay," said Windflower. "I'm heading over to the Mug-Up for a cup of tea. If you hear anything you know how to reach me. Otherwise meet me back here later and we'll head over to see Roger Buffet."

Tizzard was gone before Windflower could change his mind about more desk duty. After reminding Betsy to call him if Genges from Forensics showed up, he headed out towards the café.

As he walked along the quiet morning streets he was pleasantly surprised to see that the sun had broken through the curtain of rain and fog. Maybe this case will start to break too, he thought.

Chapter Seventeen

Windflower poked his head into the busy café and waved hello to Sheila who smiled and waved back. He took a table near the door and ordered a mug of tea from Marie. The usual suspects were holding court in their corner of the Mug-Up and he noticed the volume level of their morning chat go considerably down as he waited for his tea.

His cell phone rang and he answered it. "Windflower".

"It's Betsy, Sergeant. I just wanted to warn you. Harvey Brenton is on his way over to meet you and he's got a full head of steam. I tried to get him to wait until you got back but he insisted on knowing where you were right now. I didn't have much choice but to tell him. Sorry about that, sir."

"Don't worry about it, Betsy," said Windflower. "I was looking to speak to Mr. Brenton myself."

Just as he put the phone back in his pocket and started to sip his strong black tea, a short, red-faced, heavy-set man with thinning gray hair stormed into the café.

Harvey Brenton, thought Windflower. He wasn't really comfortable having a public display but sometimes a situation like this will bring out the best or worst in someone, and Windflower wanted to see all sides of Harvey Brenton up close and personal.

As soon as Brenton saw Windflower he started towards his table.

"Good morning, I assume you're Harvey Brenton. My name is Sergeant Winston Windflower," said the RCMP officer.

"I know who you are," snarled Harvey Brenton. "I want to know why you guys are harassing my wife and sniffing around my house when I'm not at home."

"Well we are conducting an investigation, Mr. Brenton," Windflower replied calmly, "and if any of my officers have treated your wife disrespectfully I would like to hear about it. The RCMP certainly does not condone such behaviour."

"You know what I mean," Brenton snapped back, his red face fairly glowing as he stared at Windflower. "Guys like you are just poking around in people's business and trying to stir up trouble, like always. Why don't you go back to where you belong?"

By now every eye and ear in the café was trained on Windflower and the stocky man who was confronting him. This was the best entertainment they had witnessed in years.

Windflower chose to ignore the last remark. Having been stationed all over Canada, he knew better than to rise to the racist card. As much as Harvey Brenton was used to getting his own way he was the authority here and he had the badge and uniform to prove it.

"Mr. Brenton, maybe we should have this conversation back at the office where it is a little more private?"

"Go to hell," was Brenton's response. "And keep away from my wife, or else you'll be very sorry," he shouted as he blew out of the café.

All the regulars looked fervently at Windflower hoping for a continuation of the drama, but the Sergeant just sipped his tea and watched as Harvey Brenton's Escalade sped out of the Mug-Up parking lot.

So that was Harvey Brenton, thought Windflower. Pretty cocksure of himself and clearly a man who thought highly of himself but Windflower had dealings with men like that before and like all bullies, Mr. Brenton would back down if he was really challenged. Unless Harvey Brenton got to Inspector MacIntosh first.

Windflower dialed MacIntosh's number on his cell phone but only got his answering machine. He left a message asking him to call, waved goodbye to Sheila and started back towards the office. Just around the corner from the café Tizzard pulled up along side him in his cruiser.

"Get in Boss, Genges and the boys from St. John's are here. I told them to meet us at the Martin house."

"Thanks, Tizzard," said Windflower. "Did you talk to the cleaning lady?"

"I'm just on my way over to see her now, Sarge. Her name is Millie Foote and she lives on the other side of the bridge. I'll drop you off, talk to her, and come back to get you," said Tizzard.

They pulled up in front of the Martin house on Elizabeth Avenue where a white panel van was parked in the driveway. Several men in white coats were scurrying around like mice removing pieces of equipment from the van while a tall RCMP officer stood nearby directing traffic.

"You must be Windflower," he said, extending his hand. "I'm Bill Genges from forensics."

"Winston Windflower," said the Sergeant, reaching out to meet his hand. "Thanks for coming."

"That's our job," said Genges. "So what are we looking for?"

"I'd like your guys to take a good look around and see if you see anything unusual," replied Windflower. "But mostly I'd like to see if you can find a source of arsenic. The deceased had enough of the stuff in him to kill him, and it looks like it took a long time to take its full effect."

"Arsenic, that's a new one on me," said Genges. "But we can certainly take samples of all the food and medical products in the house and once we can get back to the lab we'll run the tests. It should only take a couple of hours to go through the house and if we get approval for overtime we can have the results back to you by Sunday night."

"The overtime is fine," said Windflower. "We need to clear this up as soon as possible. If there's any questions in St. John's, tell them to call Inspector MacIntosh. I'm sure he'll approve it."

Windflower wasn't sure of any such thing but he wasn't going to let his one chance at getting to the truth get caught up in a bureaucratic snafu at Headquarters. Besides, by the time MacIntosh got wind of it he would have his answer. He walked through the house with Genges and told him the rest of what he knew about the case and the people involved and then waited outside for Tizzard to return.

Soon he saw the speeding Tizzard coming down the road towards him. I have to speak to Tizzard about slowing down, he thought, but before he got the chance Tizzard was already nattering on about Elias Martin's housekeeper.

"Let's go see Roger Buffet, Tizzard. You can give me an update on the way," said Windflower.

Tizzard looked so longingly at the forensics team activity in the Martin house that Windflower added, "And when we're done you can come back and help out the forensic guys. Maybe you'll pick up a thing or two."

Tizzard's gleam returned and he proceeded to tell his Sergeant what he had found out from the housekeeper. "Millie Foote sounds like she's happy to be rid of her job looking after the Martin house, Sarge. She described Elias Martin as crooked as sin and he was always complaining about headaches and a bad stomach. She told him to go to the doctor but he was too stubborn to let anyone near him."

"Oh, and he was always forgetting things and blaming her for stealing his stuff. She was about to quit just before he died. She also said something very interesting. Elias Martin accused her of trying to poison him. He insisted on having her taste his food before she served him and only used the water that he carried down from the Cape to make his tea."

"Did you probe her on the poisoning angle?" asked Windflower.

"I asked her if she thought that was strange, Boss, and she replied that she thought Elias Martin was one brick short of a load," said Tizzard.

"Do you think it's possible that this woman poisoned Elias Martin, Tizzard?" asked Windflower.

"I guess anything is possible but it's hard to imagine Aunt Millie hurting a fly. She has been a housekeeper for dozens of families over the years and as far as I know there have never been any problems with her. I guess forensics will help us determine the source of the poisoning, won't they, and if it's in any of the food that Millie Foote prepared we'll have our answer."

"Don't get too far ahead of yourself, Constable," said Windflower as they pulled up in front of the detachment. "Millie Foote had the means and opportunity. Until we can rule her out she has to be considered." Now let's see what Mr. Roger Buffet has to say for himself this fine morning."

The Buffet house was a small bungalow on the coastline at the far end of town with a smaller fishing shack behind it. The clapboard was cracked from wind and rain and whatever colour paint had been on it had long faded to a vague grayish green. A few relics of better times, a rotting dory and a companion rusting motor spoke of better days.

Tizzard's sharp knock on the door brought the appearance of a large, unkempt figure in a tattered housecoat. "Good morning, Mrs. Buffet. This is my Boss, Sergeant Winston Windflower, said Tizzard.

"Morning, ma'am," said Windflower.

"He's still abed," Mrs. Buffet answered. "You can try and get him up but he won't get up for me."

Tizzard nodded to the lady and headed off into the back rooms to rouse Roger Buffet. Mrs. Buffet ignored Windflower and went back to the living room to watch TV with her cup of tea.

Soon Windflower could hear rough noises coming from the bedroom area and a gruff voice letting Tizzard know exactly what he thought of being awakened from his morning lay-in.

"C'mon Roger. We haven't got all day," Windflower heard his young constable say.

"Hold your frigging horses, you arsehole," was part of the reply. But sooner rather than later Tizzard re-emerged with an unshaven and shaky Roger Buffet.

"Good morning, Mr. Buffet," said Windflower. "We want to ask you a few questions about Elias Martin."

"Elias Martin, that bastard!!" sputtered Buffet. "I'm glad he's dead and I hope he rots in hell." He rose and went to the fridge and grabbed a bottle of beer. But before he could open it, Tizzard took it from his hands.

"Not til we're done here," he told the older man. Buffet muttered at Tizzard but sat down at the kitchen table.

Windflower pulled up a chair beside him and looked him directly in the eyes. "You didn't like Elias Martin much did you?" he asked.

"I hated his guts," said Buffet. "I'm glad he's dead. He took my son and in my book it's an eye for an eye. Now you can stay or you can go but I'm having a beer." And with that he got up and went back to the fridge to retrieve his beer bottle. Tizzard went to stop him but Windflower just silently nodded no.

"Mr. Buffet, did you kill Elias Martin?" asked Windflower. But by now Roger Buffet was in the process of emptying his first beer of the day and on his way to the second. He made no reply to Windflower's question.

"Let's go," said Windflower to Tizzard. "Thank you for your time, Mr. Buffet," he said. But again Buffet ignored him in favour of his drink of choice. In the car, Tizzard said "I guess he's still on the list, isn't he Boss?"

"Let's see what forensics turns up," was Windflower's brief response as they drove the rest of the way back to the detachment in silence. "Why don't you go back to the Martin house and I'll catch up with you there in a while?"

"Okay, Sarge," said Tizzard and Windflower watched as he spun the car out of the parking lot and raced up the street. I have to talk to that boy, thought Windflower, before he kills somebody, or himself.

Windflower briefly noticed a brand new light blue Buick Enclave in front of the building but quickly passed into the detachment office. Betsy's wide eyes immediately alerted him that something was going on.

"She's in your office, Sergeant," whispered Betsy.

"Who's in my office?" whispered back Windflower.

"Marge Brenton," said Betsy.

Chapter Eighteen

Well this is a surprise, thought Windflower, especially after my conversation with her husband this morning. He went into the office to greet his visitor.

"Good morning, Mrs. Brenton, I'm Sergeant Winston Windflower." He knew that Marge Brenton had to be in her late sixties but she looked ten years younger than that. She was tall and slender and still quite an attractive woman. Well preserved was what came to mind.

Only the wrinkles around her eyes and at the corners of her mouth revealed a hint of her real age. Her hands showed little signs of normal aging as she clutched her purse in her lap. Probably some expensive anti-aging cream thought Windflower. Her light brown mohair coat hung over the back of her chair, perfectly matching her tan leather skirt and white frilly blouse. Long-sleeved, noted Windflower, which seemed a bit much for the mild weather they'd been having. A beautiful, white silk scarf with tiny brown diamonds hung over her shoulders.

Her hair was clearly professionally styled and sparkled silvery gray in the sunlight that streamed in through the window. But it was Marge Brenton's eyes that caught and held Windflower's attention. They were hazel green and almost glowed as she rose to greet him.

"Good morning, Sergeant," she said in a surprisingly strong lilting voice. "I need to talk to you about Elias Martin."

"Does your husband know you're here?" asked Windflower thinking back to his conversation with Harvey Brenton at the café.

"No, and I'd prefer that he didn't," she replied. Me too, thought Windflower.

"No one needs to know anything," replied Windflower.

"Good," she said. "My husband has a bit of a temper and I'd really rather not have another row with him about this."

"Another row," noted Windflower to himself.

"Go on Mrs. Brenton," said Windflower deciding to let her tell him first whatever she came for before he started questioning her.

"Elias was a great friend to me, Sergeant. Is it true what people are saying that he was poisoned?" she asked.

"We believe that poisoning was a direct contribution to Mr. Martin's death," replied Windflower, deciding to be upfront in the hopes of generating as much information as possible from the lady in front of him.

"Dear God!" said Marge Brenton, pulling a monogrammed handkerchief out of her purse, and dabbing at her eyes.

Windflower paused to allow her to regain her composure and then prompted her to go on by saying "You said you wanted to talk to me about Elias Martin."

"Yes, Sergeant," she replied, having regained her emotional balance. "Elias and I go back a long ways. Almost since we were children. He was so nice to me when I first moved to Frenchman's Cove and I didn't really know anybody. He was always a gentleman. One of the hardest things in my life was when he moved away. Of course I understood why he was doing it. My family wanted me to have the finer things in life and he certainly was never going to be able to provide those."

"Was it your choice to marry Harvey Brenton?" asked Windflower.

"Nobody has ever made me do anything that I didn't want to do, and nobody ever will," she responded coolly. "I was young but could see that Harvey Brenton could give me things that I could never have with Elias. It was a simple choice."

"After we were both married we didn't have much contact for a while, except for a card at Christmas and wakes and funerals. Harvey, of course forbade all connections between us, but that wasn't the reason. I just didn't want to hurt Elias any more than I already had. Besides he had a lovely woman, Eileen, and I just hoped and prayed that he would be happy."

"Were you happy, Mrs. Brenton?" Windflower asked softly.

"I had a beautiful home, could travel where and when I wanted, and when the children came along I felt satisfied to just be a mother. Harvey is not exactly the prince of personality but he was a good provider and left me alone to run the household as I saw fit. I could have been very much worse off, Sergeant."

"When did you start having contact with Elias Martin again, Mrs. Brenton?" asked Windflower.

"I guess it was probably ten years or so after I was married. I came to Grand Bank to visit an old friend and happened to run into Elias and Eileen at a church dinner one night. He was a perfect gentleman and Eileen was such a great person. They seemed happy together and I was happy for Elias. We stayed in contact after that and whenever I visited the area I would drop in on them for a cup of tea."

"Did your husband know about these visits?" asked Windflower.

"Eventually he found out but I wasn't really trying to hide anything, Sergeant. Harvey did his usual blowhard, forbidding routine and I just listened to him and went on doing what I wanted," she replied. "I may have been married to him but he didn't own me. When Eileen got sick I started coming by more regularly, every couple of weeks, to bring a pot of soup or a loaf of home-made bread. Eileen was a saint with what she went through and Elias was heartbroken. When she finally died it was like the life got sucked out of him too."

"Elias would call me often during those days and many nights I would listen to him cry. But he got through it as we all can and while he never really regained his spark he was doing quite well. He and I had become close again through this ordeal and I often shared things with him that I couldn't talk about with anyone else. But then Harvey caught me talking to Elias one night and all hell broke loose. Harvey not only forbade me from talking to Elias but came over here to see him."

"What did your husband say to Elias Martin, Mrs. Brenton?" asked Windflower.

"He told him that he would kill him if didn't stay away from me," replied Marge Brenton.

Chapter Nineteen

"Do you think he was serious, Mrs. Brenton?" asked Windflower.

"Harvey was and is a serious man," she replied. Windflower thought back to his morning conversation and had to agree with her.

"But Harvey's temper was short and fast, Sergeant Windflower. He would be furious one day but have forgotten about it by the next morning. That's the only way I have managed to live with him for all these years."

"Harvey was jealous of what Elias and I had, Sergeant, but I can't believe he'd kill him. He just wanted to do what he always does, scare people away from what he believed was his. I would have never left him for Elias. I loved them both, but I had long since made my choice. And both of them knew it."

"Elias was a dear soul, even in the last months when he started to lose it. He was kind and gentle and we deeply cared for each other. But we were just friends." At this last statement Marge Brenton began to cry softly and Windflower handed her the box of Kleenex from the credenza near his desk.

He paused to let her regain her composure and then asked "Was he sick for very long, Mrs. Brenton?"

"Elias had a series of complaints, like we all do as we get up there in age, but he talked most recently about his stomach problems and said that he often felt dizzy. He also complained about his feet bothering him, which was strange for Elias who spent most of his life tramping around the country. I offered to take him over to the clinic several times but he wouldn't hear of it. It seemed that he felt like he had to go through the same pain that his Eileen had. It was sad to see him suffer like that," said Mrs. Brenton.

"When was the last time you saw him, Mrs. Brenton?" asked Windflower.

"Three weeks ago," she replied. "I've been away to Boston to visit my sister and just got back on the weekend."

"Thank you, Mrs. Brenton. You have been really helpful."

"You're welcome, Sergeant Windflower," she replied. "Since I am the only witness to many of these conversations that we've talked about I would appreciate your discretion in keeping them confidential. There's not much point in dragging all of this up now, is there? Elias is dead, and besides, I will never speak badly about my husband in public. I just thought that someone needed to know the truth."

"I understand Mrs. Brenton. Unless there is some need directly related to the investigation I don't see why this information is in the public interest," replied Windflower.

"Thank you Sergeant," said a newly composed and confident Marge Brenton and she shook his hand and rose to leave.

As Marge Brenton drove off in her shiny new car, Windflower thought that there was one strong lady. He reflected on what she had said about her husband. What bothered him was that although Harvey Brenton was certainly a man with the potential for violence, he didn't appear to be somebody with the patience to wait for somebody to die before he got his revenge. Then again, passion was a strong motivator that made people do strange, out-of-character things. For now Harvey Brenton was a prime suspect. Unfortunately all he had was jealousy as a motive.

And of course the scarf. If Windflower believed Marge Brenton, which he did, then the scarf he found on the Cape was probably not hers. But whose was it? Someone wearing a brown scarf had been up there close to the time of Elias Martin's last morning walk, but who? At this point he had no answers to that question.

To take his mind off this continuing question Windflower decided to delve into the other joys of police work and dumped the overflowing contents of his in-box onto his desk. A good first step might be to divide it into piles, he thought, so he started amassing mini-heaps of duty reports, traffic investigations, policy and procedure memos from headquarters, assorted brochures, and what looked like real correspondence into separate sections on his desk. He quickly read and initialed the duty reports and traffic investigations and dumped the brochures into his wastepaper basket.

Exhausted from this avalanche of paper burdens he left the rest neatly stacked on his desk and wandered out to hand over his completed portions to Betsy. But Betsy had apparently gone off to lunch leaving Windflower and his thoughts alone in the office.

Might as well head back over to the Martin house to see how Genges and the forensic boys were making out. He drove there quickly and arrived just as the group was breaking up for lunch.

"Where are you guys headed?" asked Windflower.

"I thought I'd take them over to the fish and chips place in Fortune," said Tizzard. "Let the townies get some real fresh fish for a change."

Genges and the other members of the forensics team laughed at Tizzard's joke and Genges said "Why don't you come along Sergeant?"

"That's a great idea, why don't you jump in with me and Tizzard can take the rest of the gang?"

The day continued to be sunny and bright even as they crept over the hills toward Fortune and Windflower thought at least I'll have a few pleasant moments in what was already becoming a very trying day.

Soon all five of them were sitting on the picnic benches enjoying fresh fish and chips with lots of salt and malt vinegar to spice it up. As he ate his heaping portion of food Windflower thought to himself, "We could just as well be any group of office or construction workers out for lunch. Except that the guys in the white suits examined dead bodies and crime scenes and sooner or later I'll have to catch whoever is responsible."

Chapter Twenty

Windflower gave Genges a lift back to the Martin house after lunch and along the way got to chat with the forensics inspector about how their investigation was going. Staff Sergeant Bill Genges was a friendly, affable man, based in St. John's but originally from the northern Newfoundland community of St. Anthony. He was happy to chat about his work with another Mountie.

"So how did you get into forensics?" asked Windflower.

"I was stationed in Truro when a course came up in Ottawa," said Genges. "I volunteered and got sent up to HQ for six months and when I came back I was assigned to the Nova Scotia forensics unit."

"I guess I've always had an interest in science. I got my BSc from Acadia a few years back but never figured out what to do with it so I just joined the force. Forensics seemed a good fit although today forensics is more about technology than science."

"What do you mean?" asked Windflower.

"Well there's still some measuring and evaluation but nowadays we are able to do most investigations in the field using things like thermal scanning and DNA matching right from our lab in St. John's," said Genges.

"Can you get a DNA match from hair?" asked Windflower.

"Sure," said Genges. "All we need is a single strand to identify the DNA. But it's up to you to give us the match."

"What else can you get DNA from?" asked Windflower, ignoring the fact that he was no way near having anybody to match a sample to.

"Teeth, bones, skin or any body fluid like blood, semen or saliva," answered Genges. "Got a suspect?"

"I've got a few ideas but nothing firmed up yet. I'm hoping you guys can make the picture a little clearer," said Windflower.

He dropped Genges back at the Martin house and headed back to the detachment to pick up the scarf in his desk. I just hope that the wind and all my handling of this evidence haven't screwed it up, he thought.

He arrived at the detachment, waved hello and goodbye to a puzzled Betsy, grabbed the plastic bag with the scarf and headed back to the Martin house. When he arrived Genges was standing outside with one of his technicians. They were poring over something beside the house.

"Hey, Sergeant, come over here and have a look at what Brownie has found." Genges held up one of the water containers in his gloved hand and showed it to Windflower. "See anything strange?" he asked.

All Windflower could see was an empty plastic water jug. "Looks like an empty jug to me," said Windflower.

"This is why they pay us the big bucks," said Genges. "When Brown put his ultraviolet light over this jug he noticed a small abnormality." He pointed out what looked to Windflower like a pin prick hole on the top of the container, just underneath the handle.

"Brownie saw this right away, except the hole was covered the first time he looked. He picked a little at the surface and lo and behold look what we have here," said Genges.

"It was probably some kind of crazy glue," said Brown who was clearly pleased to be the center of his Boss's attention. "Whoever made the hole filled it back in, hoping nobody would notice. I've checked all the other containers, sir, and they've all got the same markings."

"The purpose of the hole, Brownie?" asked Genges.

"Well we can't be sure until we get back to the lab but I would guess that the hole was made by a pointy object, a pin or a needle, with the purpose of putting something into these containers besides water, sir," he replied.

"Good work, Brownie," said Genges. "Gather up all these containers and give them to Tizzard. We'll take a couple back with us for further testing."

As Brown picked up the water jugs Genges smiled at Windflower. "You may just have your means Windflower," he said.

"Maybe," said Windflower, "assuming that there is evidence of arsenic in these containers."

"We'll know that by Sunday," replied Genges.

"Can you also see if there are any other fingerprints on these water jugs besides Elias Martin's?" asked Windflower.

"We can do that right away," said Genges and called out to his technician. "Brownie, can you take all these containers into the van and dust them for prints? We're trying to see if there are more than one set of prints on them besides the deceased."

Turning back to Windflower he said "It might be difficult to get a good set of prints off these containers. They've been outside in the wind and weather for God knows how long but it's worth a shot. Good thinking, Sergeant, you might have a career in forensics ahead of you."

Windflower laughed. "I'm just trying to get through this case. Here's what I want you to have a look at for hair and see what you come up with." He handed Genges the bag with the scarf in it.

Genges carefully took the scarf and put into a larger evidence bag. "We'll see what we can do. We've got another hour or so here and then we'll pack up and head back. Anything else you want us to check out?"

"No, that's it for now. You've been very helpful," said Windflower. "Let me know about the prints, okay?"

"Will do," said Genges.

"Is my boy Tizzard still hanging around?" asked Windflower.

"He's inside soaking up the CSI atmosphere," laughed Genges. "I'll send him out."

Tizzard came out looking flushed and not a little disappointed to be taken away from the action. "Yes, Sarge?" he asked.

"I want you to stay here and help forensics to clean up and then re-secure the site. They're also going to give you some materials that I want you to label and store in the evidence room."

"No problem," said Tizzard, happy to be playing a real part in the crime scene investigation.

"Before you come back I also want you to do another quick round with the neighbours. Don't tell them anything but ask if they have noticed any visitors to this house in the last week or so.

"OK, Sarge," said Tizzard. "I'll report back in later."

"Great", said Windflower. "I'm heading back to the office. If you need me I'll be there."

As Windflower drove slowly back to the RCMP detachment he opened the cruiser's window to let in the late spring breeze. Things were definitely looking up. He had a suspect with a strong motive and a possible means of carrying out the deed. Now I just need to prove it, he thought.

Chapter Twenty-One

The pieces of the story were starting to come together, but before Windflower could make a case against either Roger Buffet or Harvey Brenton, he needed some more information and a little luck, maybe, a lot of luck, he thought.

Back at the detachment he called Betsy into his office. "I need you to some digging around for me," he said.

"What would you like me to do, Sergeant?" she asked.

"First I'd like to see any files we have on Elias Martin, Roger Buffet and Harvey Brenton. Not just charges but any complaints or investigations they may have been involved with in the last ten years," said Windflower. He knew that sometimes informal records were kept when there were investigations but no formal charges. They weren't part of the official record but every detachment office had its unofficial sources as well. And Betsy knew where they all were.

"I'd also like you to get me a list of companies and properties that Harvey Brenton owns or operates," he said. "You can start with the Commercial Crime section in St. John's. If they don't have the information they can tell you where you can get it. I'd also like to know what type of activities his companies are engaged in and if the Commercial section has a file on Harvey Brenton."

"When do you want this information?" asked Betsy.

"I'd like to have it by tomorrow if possible, Betsy," he answered.

"Okay, I'll see what I can find out," she replied. "And Constable Tizzard left a number for the Grandys in St. John's for you. Here is it," as she handed him a slip of paper.

"Thanks, Betsy," said Windflower as she left to begin her task.

Now to find out a little more about arsenic. I guess I should have done this before, thought Windflower, as his computer powered up, but better late than never. His first stop, Wikipedia. Not usually the most reliable source of information for a police officer but in this case a great place to start.

What Windflower found out was that arsenic and its compounds are used as pesticides, herbicides, insecticides and in various alloys. He also noted wryly that arsenic has a long history of being used for murder and that because of its use by the ruling class to murder one another, arsenic has been known as the Poison of Kings and the King of Poisons.

But the most interesting thing that Windflower found out about arsenic was that because of its toxicity to insects, bacteria, and fungi, arsenic was used as a wood preserver since the 1950's. As more information about the dangers of arsenic became known this practice was banned in the European Union and the United States, and eventually in Canada. But that wasn't until 2004 and any construction company that had been around since that time would certainly have access to a ready supply of arsenic.

That means Harvey Brenton would likely have access as well as anybody who worked on a construction site. Windflower made a note to ask Tizzard to see if Roger Buffet had recently worked construction as well. Just then the phone rang, snapping Windflower out of the fantasy world of the Internet and back to real life.

"Windflower," he answered.

"Winston, it's Bill Genges. We're just packing up to go but I thought you'd like to know that we found at least two sets of readable prints on those water containers. And a very nice thumb print right over those little holes in two of them. I've given one container to Tizzard to bring back to you and I'll take the other one to the lab in St. John's."

"That is good news, Bill," said Windflower. "Can you tell by the size of the prints whether they are from a man or a woman?"

"Well I guess it is possible they could be either, but it would have to be a pretty big woman with incredibly large hands in order for them to belong to a woman. The law of probabilities says that these prints are from two men. One of them is likely the deceased which you should get matched before the funeral and the other one is....," Genges paused and let Windflower finish the line.

"Not quite sure yet, but at least I've got possibilities," said Windflower.

"Don't forget, Winston, the Mounties always get their man," laughed Genges.

"Thanks for all your help on this, Bill," said Windflower, "and call me on my cell phone anytime you get results from the testing."

"No problem, Sergeant, I'll give you a call on Sunday."

As Genges hung up Windflower allowed himself a brief smile. Maybe I will get my man (or woman) after all.

He heard a car pull up in the parking lot and saw Tizzard struggling out of his patrol car burdened down by boxes and bags of what must be evidence from the Martin house. Better give him a hand, thought Windflower.

"Thanks, Sarge," said Tizzard as he off-loaded half of his pile to Windflower.

"Let's get this stuff into the evidence room," said Windflower.

Once the boxes and water containers had been tagged and secured, Tizzard and Windflower sat in the back room to debrief.

"Did you talk to the neighbours?" asked Windflower.

"I didn't get them all but Mavis Emberley told me something very interesting", said Tizzard, pulling out his notebook. "Last week she remembered seeing a woman in a brown scarf going into the Martin house and then walking up to the Cape."

"Did she have a description?" asked Windflower

"She said that the woman was short and stout with a long gray coat," quoting from his notes. "That might have been Harvey Brenton, Sarge."

Chapter Twenty-Two

"It might have been, Tizzard. It just might have been", said Windflower. "Or it might have been Roger Buffet or even Marge Brenton. And we haven't even talked to the Grandy's yet. Don't get too far ahead of yourself, Tizzard."

"We're a long ways from accusing Harvey Brenton of anything other than being a pompous ass at this point," said Windflower. "But he is an interesting suspect. Until we get more evidence we are in no position to prove anything against anyone."

"But if Harvey Brenton's fingerprints are on the water jugs, and if the jugs have been tampered with, and if that 'woman' in the scarf was really him, then we've got him," said Tizzard.

"That's three ifs and a but," said Windflower, "none of which we can prove."

Tizzard, looking a little dejected had to agree. "So how do we prove all of this?"

"The first step," said Windflower "is to get a firm confirmation on Elias Martin's fingerprints. Where is he being waked?"

"He's at Pike's Funeral Home," said Tizzard.

"Can you go over there after visiting hours tonight and take Mr. Martin's fingerprints? Call ahead before you go and let them know you're coming, but don't go until everybody has left for the evening, and don't let anyone see you doing it, okay?"

"Okay, Sarge," said Tizzard, happy to be doing what looked like real detective work.

"You know how to take fingerprints, don't you, Tizzard?" asked Windflower.

"Sure," laughed Tizzard, "it was my favourite part of the training program."

"Just don't screw it up," said Windflower with a smile. "And while you're waiting why don't you see if you can find out what Roger Buffet has been doing for money in recent years? He's clearly not been fishing by the looks of his boat. See if he has been working in the construction industry, will you?"

Tizzard nodded and left humming to himself as Windflower glanced at his watch. 4:45. I guess we can call it a day. Saying goodnight to Tizzard and Betsy Windflower grabbed his coat and hat and headed home.

On the way through the back streets that led to his house Windflower could feel the cool fog start to creep under his jacket as it rolled in from the water. Within an hour the whole town would be bathed in an eerie glow as the sun started to fade and the fog and the night battled for domination. Let them fight it out he thought. I just want a quiet evening at home.

He picked up his mail at the post office and stopped by the corner grocery for some fresh carrots and onions and the latest issue of the local rag, the Southern Gazette. It didn't have a lot of news but he liked to know what was going on in his community. He nodded hello to a few of the walking ladies who smiled as he passed them on the narrow streets. He arrived home, unlocked the door and was grateful for the silence that soon enveloped him. He pulled a cold beer from the fridge and laid out the newspaper on the kitchen table. Ten minutes and half the beer later he was completely up to date with all the births, deaths, marriages, engagements and fund-raising activities in his neck of the woods.

Then he spread out his stack of mail to go through. He usually only picked up his mail once a week so it was the usual hodgepodge of supermarket flyers, junk mail, bills, and sometimes even a real live letter. This week he was especially lucky, a postcard and a letter.

The letter was from his Auntie Marie who was his late mother's sister and wrote him a couple of times a year to give him the latest news from Pink Lake. Old Uncle Joe has finally passed on after his bout with cancer and it seemed like all of his cousins were married and having babies. A not too subtle hint from Auntie Marie.

She also told him about the celebrations in his home town, like last month's Spring pow-wow. He could almost taste the bannock and smoked venison and the Saskatoon berry pie as he read her words. It reminded him how much he missed his family and their times together. It also reminded him to write back to his Auntie which he did right away. Not that he had any great news, but he hoped to get back home in the fall for a visit during deer hunting season. That, he knew, would please his old Auntie.

He almost forgot about the postcard when it fell out from underneath the envelope he was addressing to his Auntie Marie. The picture was a beautiful young Hopi dancer with brilliant feathers and equally dazzling face paint. He turned it over and saw that it was from La Mesa, Arizona.

So that's where she is now, thought Windflower. Anne-Marie Littlechild, the woman he once had been engaged to, was teaching Native American art therapy on a reservation in Arizona. He and Anne-Marie had tried to make their relationship work but his desire to be an RCMP officer had forced too many separations, and finally she had given up. They had parted on good terms but she just wasn't prepared to commit to being his tag-along partner as he traversed the country. She had her own dreams to follow.

She was doing well in La Mesa, at least that's what the postcard said and Windflower was glad for that. She was a beautiful woman with a beautiful spirit. Maybe he had made a big mistake.

Mistake or not, she was in sunny, hot Arizona and he was in damp, cold, foggy Newfoundland. But he had a right to his dreams too, didn't he?

His stomach reminded him that you can't just live on dreams alone so he started frying up some onions and garlic in a frying pan and put a pot of water on the stove to boil pasta. He took out a small container of Sheila's home-made spaghetti sauce from the freezer and chopped up some carrots while he waited for the water to boil.

When it started to bubble he put two portions of spaghetti into the pot and stirred his carrots into his now browned garlic and onions. He warmed up his sauce in the microwave and eight minutes later he was sitting at his kitchen table devouring his spaghetti with carrots, onions and garlic smothered in Sheila's thick sauce.

He finished off his meal with half of the partridge berry crumble that he noticed in the fridge and a cup of chamomile tea. He stared out his kitchen window but could only see fog and more fog. Soon the fog settled over him too and although it was only 9 o'clock and the night was still young, the only partying he could think about involved a hard bed and a soft pillow.

Chapter Twenty-Three

When he awoke at seven it came to him right away. How could he have been so stupid? He searched through his jacket pockets to find Bill Genges' phone number. It might be too early to call but he wanted Genges to run the prints he had found on the water containers through the system to see what he could find out. Maybe there was already a match for one of these prints in the database.

By eight he was at his desk and on the phone to Bill Genges. No answer so he left a message.

"Bill, it's Windflower. Can you run the prints that you found at the Martin house through the system? Maybe something or someone will turn up. Can you let me know if you find anything? Thanks."

Betsy walked into his office as he hung up the phone. "Good morning, Sergeant," she said.

"Morning, Betsy. Any news on the Brenton file I asked you about?" asked Windflower.

"Nothing yet, sir, but there are some messages for you, including one from the Inspector. He said he's going to come by this morning to see you," she answered.

"Thanks, Betsy. I'd like to talk to Inspector MacIntosh. I'm going to head over to the funeral first but I should be back around 10:30," he replied.

"Any progress on the case, Sergeant?" asked Betsy.

"I think we are making some headway," said Windflower. "We'll know a little more when we hear back from forensics."

"That's very good, sir," said Betsy as she left to start her own daily routine.

I think so too, thought Windflower thumbing through his yellow message slips. Another phone call from the mayor. Man, this guy is persistent, he thought. Seeing nothing else that couldn't wait he grabbed his coat and hat and walked over to the church. By the time he arrived the hearse from Pike's Funeral Home had already arrived and the pall bearers were solemnly carrying the remains of the late Elias Martin into the church.

Windflower quietly slipped into the church and spotted Tizzard in one of the back rows. He nodded a silent good morning and sidled up beside him.

"Morning, Sarge," whispered Tizzard. "I got the prints last night. Small turnout, eh?"

Windflower glanced around at the nearly empty church and quickly counted two dozen participants at Elias Martin's farewell. There were a few neighbours, a couple of old-timers from the wharf, and in the front row an older lady and a tall young man. Georgette Sheridan and her son thought Windflower. Sitting a couple of rows behind her, by herself was an impeccably dressed Marge Brenton.

I wonder what Harvey Brenton thinks about that, thought Windflower. Sheila was there too, of course, and when he caught her eye she flashed him a very brief but warm smile. He also saw Dr. Sanjay dressed nattily in his best suit in the row behind Sheila. He was waving so frantically that Windflower had to wave back, just to get him to stop.

The Minister droned on and on about what a good life Elias Martin had lived and how now he was going to his eternal reward. Soon enough for Windflower that was over and the solemn black-dressed men from Pike's were leading the casket and the mourners back out into the morning air. Georgette Sheridan had her head down and didn't raise it to acknowledge Windflower but Marge Brenton gave him a furtive good morning nod.

Windflower followed the procession out of the church and went over to see Georgette Sheridan to express his condolences.

"Good morning, Mrs. Sheridan. I'm Sergeant Winston Windflower. Once again, I am very sorry for your loss."

"Thank you, Sergeant. This is my son, James," she replied.

"Is it true that my uncle was poisoned?" asked the young man.

"It appears so," said Windflower.

"Any idea who might have done it yet?" he further questioned Windflower.

"We're still following up on that."

"I hope you get the bastard soon," he replied.

"James, such language," reproached his mother.

"I mean it, Mom. Whoever did this to Uncle Elias was a bastard and I want him to pay," said the son.

"We'll do our best, ma'am," said Windflower as he took his leave to allow the other mourners to speak to Mrs. Sheridan. Dr. Sanjay approached him as he stood silently on the church steps.

"Good morning, Winston, a penny for your thoughts," said the doctor.

"I'm not sure they're worth even that," laughed Windflower. "How is the good doctor this morning?"

"If I felt any better, I'd be dead," the doctor joked back. "So how's the detective work going?"

"It's slow, Doc, but I think we're getting somewhere. Although I'm not quite sure where that is yet. You've been around here for a few years now, you must know Harvey Brenton. What do you know about him?"

"I have to admit that I don't know him very well. I think he goes to St. John's for his medical needs. But I think he has an anger problem. His wife is a patient of mine and without divulging too much personal information there have been incidents where that anger has, let's just say, surfaced from time to time."

"Is that so," said Windflower. "Somehow, I'm not surprised. Thanks, Doc. Enjoy the rest of the day."

"Bye, Winston, you too," said Dr. Sanjay as he headed for his car.

Just as he was leaving the church steps Windflower saw Harvey Brenton's Escalade starting to pull out of the parking lot with Marge Brenton in the front seat beside her husband. He thought he saw a scowl on Harvey Brenton's face as he looked towards him, but maybe that was Brenton's natural look.

Tizzard came up to Windflower as he was watching the SUV pull away. "They say that the murderer always shows up at the funeral, Boss," he said.

"You've been watching too much TV, Tizzard," said Windflower. "Let's go for a cup of coffee. MacIntosh is coming to see me this morning and I need to clear my head before he takes it off."

On the way to the Mug-Up Windflower's cell phone rang. "Windflower," he answered.

"It's Bill Genges, Sergeant. I've got good news for you. There's a match on one of the two sets of fingerprints, and it's not the late Mr. Martin."

"Who is it?" asked Windflower.

"Well your boy's name is Patrick Cormier," said Genges. "Originally from Montreal he's got a lengthy record from assault to armed robbery to smuggling drugs. Did four years in Millhaven for the armed robbery and another five in Joliet on the drug charges. His latest arrest was for assault causing bodily harm, right around the corner from you in Marystown. Beat a guy senseless with a pool cue. The investigators thought it was tied to a drug debt, but the victim wasn't prepared to testify."

"Oh yeah, one more thing. We found a couple of hairs in that scarf you gave me. They appeared to be gray. We can do the DNA test anytime you want as long as you have a possible match to give me to compare," concluded Genges.

"Thanks, Bill, that's great," said Windflower. "I'll get back to you when we get something else."

"Okay, talk to you on Sunday," said Genges as he hung up.

"So what's up, Sarge?" asked Tizzard.

"I'll tell you when I get my coffee," said Windflower.

Chapter Twenty-Four

Windflower directed Tizzard to a quiet corner table while he went to the counter to place his order. But mostly he just wanted to say hello to Sheila who was also just back from the funeral.

"Good morning, Sheila, how are you?" he asked.

"Just fine, thank you Sergeant, what can I do for you?" She smiled back.

"Two cups of coffee and two of those nice raisin tea buns you make, thanks Sheila."

"I'll bring them right over," she said with a twinkle.

Windflower was still smiling when he got back to the table with Tizzard, til he saw the silly grin on the constable's face.

"Okay, Tizzard, there's been another twist in the case," said Windflower suddenly turning serious and hoping his younger companion would do the same.

Tizzard's eyes immediately lit up and he almost stood at attention while sitting up in his chair.

"The second set of prints on the water containers belong to a Patrick Cormier. He's got a criminal record for armed robbery and drugs. He's also up for assault in Marystown."

"What's his connection to the case, Sarge?" asked Tizzard.

"Well, based on his fingerprints he just got moved up the suspect list," said Windflower. "As far as motive goes it's hard to figure out though. He doesn't sound like the kind of guy to take this type of initiative on his own."

"Maybe someone put him up to it," said Tizzard.

"Maybe," said Windflower, "but until we talk to him we don't know anything for sure, except that his fingerprints were on what might be a murder weapon. I want you to call Marystown and find out where he is now. If he's out on bail awaiting trial then have them pick him up and hold him until we can go and get him. Then I want you to bring him back over here so we can have a chat with him. Also, see if you can find out from Marystown what he has been up to lately, who he hangs around with, where he works. Whatever you can find out. Don't tell the Marystown guys what you want with Cormier, just that your Sergeant told you it's part of an on-going investigation. I don't want Cormier or anyone else spooked before they get him safely over here. Understood?"

"Got it Boss," said Tizzard.

Just then Sheila came by with their coffee and tea buns.

"Here you go, gentlemen," she said.

"Thanks", they said in unison and opened the steaming tea buns so that they could spread fresh butter all over them.

"Nice to see men with appetites," said Sheila. "Good for business." She laughed.

"Don't worry, we'll be back," said Windflower.

They devoured their snack and lingered just a little sipping their coffee.

Finally Tizzard broke the silence with a question that had been on both their minds since the subject of Cormier had come up. "Where does this leave Harvey Brenton?" he asked his Sergeant.

"Right now, nowhere," said Windflower. "I'm going to do a little more digging around but unless some other evidence turns up or we can find a connection between Cormier and Brenton, he might be in the clear."

Tizzard looked greatly disappointed and said "I guess you're right but my gut still tells me that he's involved somehow."

Windflower felt the same but simply said, "Let's get Cormier over here and see what he has to say for himself. In the meantime I need to talk to Ches Grandy and you need to find out what kind of work Roger Buffet has been doing. We need to make sure that we cover all the bases."

"Okay," said Tizzard, sounding less than excited and he headed up to the counter to pay for their coffee break.

Windflower waved goodbye to Sheila and went back to Tizzard's patrol car. When they got back to the detachment Inspector MacIntosh's staff car was parked outside with a very impatient senior officer inside.

"Morning, Inspector," said Windflower.

"So what have you got?" asked MacIntosh not bothering with morning pleasantries.

"We're making some progress," said Windflower and proceeded to tell MacIntosh about the water containers and his big news about Patrick Cormier.

"I know about Cormier, he's a mean son of a bitch," said MacIntosh. "He nearly killed a guy a couple of months ago. It would be good to get him out of Marystown and off the street for good."

"We're not there yet," said Windflower. "We're still awaiting confirmation from forensics but I've asked Tizzard to get Marystown to help find him and bring him back here for questioning."

"Great," said MacIntosh, coming as close to a smile as he was capable of. "I'll call Marystown before I head back to tell them to give you and Tizzard their full cooperation."

"Thank you, Inspector," said Windflower.

"Now maybe you can stop poking your nose into the affairs of the other innocent citizens of the community," said MacIntosh.

"Well, we still have some checking to do on Roger Buffet and I have to talk to Ches Grandy but unless we have any reason to think otherwise, Cormier is our main man at this point," said Windflower.

"Good. Make sure it stays that way and keep me posted on any and all developments," said MacIntosh as he picked up the phone to call the Marystown detachment.

After MacIntosh had gone Windflower called Betsy into his office on the intercom.

"So any news, Betsy?" asked Windflower.

"Here are the files that you asked for on Roger Buffet but there is nothing on Harvey Brenton that I could find," Betsy replied.

That's strange, thought Windflower. Not even a scrap of paper on Mr. Harvey Brenton. Either he was clean as a whistle or someone had been cleaning up after him.

"Commercial Crime was also very helpful, Sergeant. Here's a list of businesses that Mr. Brenton owns or has an interest in. There's no record of any charges against him but the person I spoke with said there had been a number of investigations in the past couple of years. He put me onto a Corporal Dewar who suggested that you can call him if you want any more information. Here's his direct number."

"Thanks Betsy, you did a great job," said Windflower.

"No problem," she replied clearly pleased at the compliment she received from her superior.

After Betsy left Windflower went through the typed list she had provided. It was a long list, a very long list. Heading the company list was Brenton Construction and Building Supplies.

The company had been in operation for over 30 years. They certainly would have had access to arsenic for their lumberyard, thought Windflower. Harvey Brenton's other business interests included property development, a trucking and shipping company and a string of convenience stores along with the local liquor store licenses for most of the South Coast.

Also in Harvey Brenton's portfolio were apartment buildings in Marystown and St. John's and a hotel, restaurants and bars in Marystown. Quite an empire for this part of the world, thought Windflower. One that somebody would certainly have a great stake in protecting and someone who maybe, just maybe could use a goon like Patrick Cormier to keep other people in line.

Windflower put the list aside for now and dialed the number for Corporal Dewar in Commercial Crime. MacIntosh had told him to leave innocent citizens alone but Windflower wasn't sure quite yet that he could put Harvey Brenton in that category.

Chapter Twenty-Five

"Dewar," the voice at the other end of the line answered.

"Good morning, Corporal, it's Sergeant Winston Windflower from the Grand Bank detachment. I was told that you were the man to talk to about Harvey Brenton. He's part of an on-going investigation in Grand Bank."

"Well, as I told your secretary there have been a couple of recent investigations in which Mr. Brenton's name has come up. There was one in our section and at least one other involving the drug squad," said Dewar.

"So what were you looking at Harvey Brenton for?" asked Windflower.

"Mr. Brenton has a sizable and varied business interest in your area," answered Dewar. "He came to our attention through the drug squad who has some suspicions that he was using his trucking operation to ship drugs down the eastern seaboard of the United States and then bringing cigarettes back into Newfoundland," said Dewar.

"What kind of drugs are we talking about?" asked Windflower.

"Cocaine, mostly," said Dewar. "It was thought that the drugs were coming up by sea from Columbia and then off-loaded at remote locations across the island. The drug guys thought that Brenton, or his accomplices would pick them up and then truck them along with other legitimate merchandise out of the province. Nobody was looking for cocaine to be smuggled out of Newfoundland, not then anyway, so it was easy to get them out of the province," said Dewar.

"And getting into the U.S. is not really a problem either," said Windflower. "I heard that there are about two hundred unprotected border crossings in Atlantic Canada and Quebec alone."

"That's right," said Dewar. "And until about a year ago it was just as easy to smuggle in cigarettes. It was almost the perfect operation."

"So how did Commercial Crime get involved?" asked Windflower.

"Money-laundering," said Dewar. "With all that money coming in from his illegal operations Brenton had to put the cash somewhere, so he started to funnel it back into his regular businesses and buying other properties. He had a very creative accountant but when we started going through his books it was clear that the numbers didn't add up."

"We had the accountant under the spotlight for a few days and I think we could have cracked him and Brenton, but just as we started to get close, our investigation was shut down."

"Why did that happen, Corporal?" asked Windflower.

"I'm afraid that I'm the last person to ask, Sergeant, but people here and in the drug squad felt that someone in a higher position wanted this whole situation to go away," he replied.

"Friends in high places?" asked Windflower.

"I didn't say that, Sergeant, but you can draw your own conclusions. The file hasn't been officially closed but unless we get a new lead, or some new direction, it's deader than a doornail. By the way, what are you looking at Harvey Brenton for?" asked Dewar.

"Possible involvement in a murder," said Windflower.

"Well I hope you're more successful than we were," said Dewar.

"Me too," said Windflower. "Thanks for your help."

As he hung up from Corporal Dewar Windflower reflected on what he'd just been told. Drugs, smuggling, murder? Was Harvey Brenton really capable of all that? More importantly, could Windflower actually prove his guilt and even if he did would it make any difference? Better not focus on that part, he thought, too depressing. Besides it was possible that there was a link between Cormier and Brenton and if he could get to Cormier, then maybe he could get Brenton too.

Windflower's head was spinning. Maybe a nice long walk along the water would help. Even in the damp, gray fog Windflower could feel, hear and taste the ocean. He had never known anything like this growing up in the dense woods and hard rock of Northern Alberta.

There were plenty of deep, cold-water lakes and the mighty Athabasca roared through his home country, but nothing like this vast, powerful and endless sea. Yet he felt an affinity to this great water. It calmed his soul and helped him think clearly. And right now he had to have a clear head.

Feeling refreshed from his rendezvous with the ocean he decided to continue his mini-escape from work by walking home for lunch. Not a bad life, he thought. Where else could you walk home for lunch? After a bowl of spicy tomato soup and a ham sandwich and strong tea he felt ready to restart his day.

When he arrived back at the office he returned his phone messages, including the one from the mayor, who fortunately had left for the day. Probably out on the golf course in Grand

Meadows, trying to find his balls in the fog. Ever since the nine-hole golf course had opened up near the provincial park all of these one-time fishermen and loggers had suddenly turned into Newfoundland versions of Sam Snead. It must be good for the economy, thought Windflower, and many women in the community would be grateful for an extra half day on their own.

Tizzard came into Windflower's office at his usual breakneck speed and seemingly more excited than ever. "It appears that Cormier is quite the character, Boss, and the boys in Marystown were quite helpful in filling in the details. He's lived in an apartment in Marystown for about two years and he's got two jobs. One as a truck driver with B+H Transport and another as a bouncer/manager at the Pink Lady."

"That's a strip joint, isn't it Tizzard?" asked Windflower.

"Yeah, it's right next to the Mariners Inn in Marystown. Not that I've ever been there or anything," replied Tizzard.

"Sure, Tizzard," said Windflower. "Do you have his latest address?"

"He lives in an apartment on Ville Marie Drive in Marystown," said Tizzard.

Windflower quickly scanned Harvey Brenton's business holdings on his desk and found that Cormier's apartment building was on the list. So too was B+H Transport and the Mariners Inn. Jackpot, he thought.

"Here are the connections to Harvey Brenton, Tizzard," said Windflower as he showed Tizzard the list.

"Wow," said Tizzard. "What does this mean?"

"It means that either we have a whole lot of coincidences or Mr. Brenton and Mr. Cormier are already well acquainted. Have you arranged to have Cormier picked up?" Windflower asked.

"I am just waiting for a call confirming it from Marystown," said Tizzard, "as soon as I get it I'm on the way over there."

"Great," said Windflower. "I don't want you to talk to Cormier at all on the way over. I want him to stew until he knows what it's about. Put him in the back cell and you and I will interview him together later."

"Okay, Boss," said Tizzard who went back to the main office to wait for his call.

Windflower decided to put the waiting time to good use and while he couldn't believe it, his in-basket was overflowing again. Forty-five minutes later Tizzard poked his head in to say he was on his way to Marystown to get Cormier. Apparently Cormier wasn't that happy about being picked up. That's good thought Windflower. I want him thoroughly pissed off by the time I talk to him.

Having done the minimum amount of paperwork to satisfy himself if not the RCMP, Windflower decided to go for a cup of tea at the Mug-Up while he was waiting for Tizzard to get back. Maybe he'd even get a chance to say hi to Sheila. Now that's a pleasant thought.

Chapter Twenty-Six

Windflower whistled to himself as he walked to the café. He nodded hello to the few stragglers who were making their coffee last as long as possible and caught Sheila's eye as she was cleaning up in the kitchen. She smiled and walked over to say hello.

"Good afternoon, Sergeant. This is a pleasant surprise," she said.

"The pleasure is all mine, Madam," said Windflower. "I hope you haven't forgotten about tomorrow night. I've made arrangements with the skipper of the launch to take us over around 4 and we have dinner reservations for 7:30. That will give us a little time to have a look around. I hope that's all okay with you."

"That's perfect, Winston," said Sheila switching to the non-professional since this seemed like a strictly personal visit. "I haven't been to St. Pierre for ages. We used to go over when we were kids for the cheap wine and liqueurs but I don't think I've ever been on a date there."

"Well there's always a first time," said Windflower. "I'll arrange for a taxi to pick us up at your place and take us to the boat and then pick us up around 11 when we get back. That way if we decide to have a glass of wine or two we won't have to worry about the Mounties stopping us."

"Good plan," said Sheila. "What can I get you? I just made a fresh peanut butter cheesecake. I know it's your favourite. How about a slice and a cup of tea?"

"That would be perfect, Sheila." said Windflower.

While Windflower was waiting for his cheesecake he noticed Georgette Sheridan and her son come into the café. Sheila saw them too and went over to greet Georgette and to meet her son. She was soon back at their table with two cups of coffee and two large slices of what to Windflower looked like Sheila's partridge berry crumble.

Oh, well, thought Windflower I guess condolences come before love. Funny, that was the first time that he had thought about love and Sheila in the same sentence. He had certainly felt lots of things for Sheila, but love? He'd have to think about that one some more.

Sheila broke his daydream with his steaming tea and delicious looking cheesecake. Windflower mumbled thank you and immediately dug his fork into his mid-afternoon dessert. It was all he could do to not devour it in one gulp and all his patience to slow down enough to make it last. Two minutes later only a few crumbs remained. Some men smoke, drink or chase women as their vice. Windflower's was peanut butter cheesecake.

As a very satisfied Windflower sipped his tea, James Sheridan came over to speak with him.

"I just wanted to apologize if I was rude earlier," he said. "It's just that my Uncle Elias was the last remaining relative on my mother's side and I used to come visit him here with her in the summer when I was a kid. I know a lot of people thought Uncle Elias was a bit of a grump but he and I got along great."

"No need to apologize," said Windflower. "I know it's hard to lose somebody you care about."

"I just hope you can catch the person who did this Sergeant," the young man said.

"We'll do our best," said Windflower.

After paying Sheila and thanking her properly for the great cheesecake Windflower said goodbye to the Sheridans and wished them a safe journey home. By the time he got back to the office Betsy was packing up to go home.

"Tizzard called, Sergeant. He said to tell you that he's picked up his package and is on his way back from Marystown. Do you need me for anything else?" she asked.

"No thanks, Betsy. Have a great weekend," Windflower replied.

"Okay, you too, Sergeant," said Betsy as she waved good night.

Windflower had about an hour to kill before Tizzard got back from Marystown so he decided to put his time to good use by reviewing the duty rosters for next month and making assignments to the various functions that the Grand Bank detachment was responsible for. He added a note to the town patrol assignment to double check for teenager drinkers and to call their parents if they found any.

That should at least keep the mayor happy, he thought, as long as it's not his friends who have to pick up their drunken kids. When Windflower had finished the form he made copies for everyone and put the original on Betsy's desk.

Still time to do one more thing before Tizzard got back from Marystown, he thought. Time to phone Ches Grandy in St. John's. He dialed the number from the slip on his desk and waited as the phone rang. Soon a gruff voice answered and Windflower asked to speak to Mr. Ches Grandy.

"Speaking," said the voice at the other end of the line.

"Mr. Grandy, it's Sergeant Winston Windflower of the RCMP in Grand Bank. I'm calling you because Elias Martin recently died."

"I heard that," said Ches Grandy. "I'm none too broke up about it, but it doesn't bring me any pleasure to know he's dead. I stopped caring about that old bastard a long time ago. All me and the missus cares about these days is trying to get Ginger back on her feet."

"How is she doing?" asked Windflower. He could almost hear the other man's spirits lift as he started talking about his daughter.

"She's doing great, thank God," said Grandy. "She can now walk with a cane and with her physiotherapy she seems to get stronger every day. She is a real miracle and a fighter too. We are so proud of her."

"That's great, Mr. Grandy," said Windflower. "When was the last time you saw Elias Martin?" he gently asked, finally steering the conversation to what he really wanted from Ches Grandy.

"I haven't seen that son of a bitch since he came knocking on my door in Grand Bank, trying to say he was sorry. Sorry my ass," said Grandy. "That old codger should have never been driving that night and we'll never forgive him for what he did to our Ginger. I am not a mean person, Sergeant, but I hope he rots in hell. Neither me nor the missus have been home since those days and I suspect we'll never go back again."

"Well, thank you for your time," said Windflower, "and I hope that everything keeps getting better for your daughter."

"Thanks Sergeant, that's what we pray for every day," said Grandy as he hung up the phone.

Well, thought Windflower. The Grandys had motive to kill Elias Martin, but if they haven't been to Grand Bank since their daughter's accident it was hard to see where they might have had an opportunity to do it. Ches Grandy might still be a suspect, but he just moved way down the list. He made a few notes for the file and as he was doing it he could see Tizzard's patrol car just coming into the parking lot.

Tizzard got out and opened the back door. Patrick Cormier towered over the barely 6 foot Tizzard. He was at least 6 foot 5 and close to 300 pounds. He had a large beer gut but the rest of him was all muscle. His head was shaved a shiny bald and he had a large gold earring and what looked like a dragon's head tattoo leading up his forearm into his shoulder. Despite the coolish weather he wore jeans and a tank top. Maybe that was just to show off his muscles thought Windflower but it probably also meant that Cormier was impervious to the cold. Little things wouldn't bother him. He would be a tough nut to crack.

Windflower moved back into his office so that Cormier wouldn't see him when Tizzard brought him in. Better to have some element of surprise later. Windflower could hear Cormier mutter half-French, half-English curses at Tizzard who, true to his direction, just kept moving the hand-cuffed beast to the holding cell at the rear of the detachment. When Tizzard had Cormier securely locked inside he came out to look for Windflower.

"That is one mean hombre," said Tizzard. "He never stopped yammering those curses at me since I picked him up. I'm glad he's in cuffs, I'm not sure I could have taken him down on my own. He pissed me off so much I left the cuffs on him in the cell. For his own safety of course. By the time you're ready to talk to him he'll be in a right state."

"Good," said Windflower, "that's exactly what I want."

"Oh, yeah, and I think he was asking for a lawyer, but my French is not that good," added Tizzard.

"We just want to talk to him," said Windflower. "He doesn't need a lawyer unless we're going to charge him with something. Let's let him stew for another hour or so."

Windflower spent the next hour cleaning up the rest of his paperwork and tidying up his desk while Tizzard went over to the Mug-Up for a coffee. When he came back Windflower told him to go get the prisoner and bring him to the interview room.

By the time Windflower got there a steaming Cormier was scowling at Tizzard. "Take the cuffs off, Constable," said Windflower.

Cormier rubbed his wrists where the handcuffs had dug and chafed him and turned his glare to Windflower.

"I wants my lawyer," he spat out.

"Mr. Cormier, you don't even know what we want to talk to you about, so why do you think you need a lawyer?" asked Windflower.

"Youse guys are always trying to screw around with a guy like me, just because I'm French," said Cormier.

"Well we can certainly get your lawyer if you want Mr. Cormier, but he may not be too happy to find out that you are in violation of your bail conditions by working in a strip club and associating with known criminals. Especially since he put up the bond. The judge won't be too happy either. I suspect that they'll probably want to keep you in jail until the trial, which could be a few more months. I hear the Marystown court is really busy these days," said Windflower calmly.

Tizzard's research with the guys from Marystown on Cormier's bail conditions had certainly come in helpful, thought Windflower as Tizzard winked at him from behind the prisoner.

After thinking about it for a few minutes Cormier finally relented. "Okay, okay, you bastards. What do you want?" asked Cormier.

"That's what we like to see, Mr. Cormier, cooperative citizens helping out their local police force," said Windflower as he returned Tizzard's wink.

Chapter Twenty-Seven

"So tell me how well you know Harvey Brenton," asked Windflower, going right to the point.

Looking a little surprised Cormier said "I work for Monsieur Brenton's trucking company. I drives a truck."

"How much rent do you pay at your apartment?" asked Windflower.

"My apartment is included in my salary," said Cormier. "Dey pays me extra to have a Frenchman drive the trucks here, the Newfies are too stupid or lazy," he sneered.

Windflower could see Tizzard tensing up behind Cormier but he pushed on.

"What about your job at the strip club, the Pink Lady, who pays your salary there?" asked Windflower.

"I gets the cover charge and all dey girls pays me a percentage plus extra privileges, if you knows what I mean," Cormier said smugly.

Cormier had clearly answered these types of questions before, or he had been well coached, thought Windflower. Maybe it's time for something different.

"Do you know Elias Martin?" asked Windflower.

"Is he the dead guy?" asked Cormier, "had a heart attack or something?"

"Mr. Martin is dead, that's right," said Windflower. "Did you know him or not?"

"Never met him in my life," said Cormier, once again a little too smugly for Windflower's and especially Tizzard's liking.

"When was the last time you were in Grand Bank?" Windflower asked.

"I tries not to come here," said Cormier. "This place is dey arsehole of the world. I think I was here last summer at that stupid Grand Bank Day. Got drunk and watched a bunch of stupid Newfies making fun of demselves."

"Spare us the editorial comments," said Windflower. "We found your fingerprints out at Elias Martin's house. What were you doing there?"

"Told you, don't know dey man, don't even know where he lives," said Cormier.

"Well you better come up with a better explanation than that," said Windflower. "Otherwise we are going to charge you with murder."

"Murder?" screamed Cormier standing to his full 6 foot 5. "Youse guys are trying to set me up for murder? You bastards." And pointing his finger into Windflower's face he said, "I wants my lawyer."

"Sit down Mr. Cormier. Constable Tizzard will take you out to make your phone call. We'll leave the cuffs off unless you start any trouble. You're not going to cause any trouble, are you Mr. Cormier?"

Cormier just scowled and followed Tizzard out into the main office to phone his lawyer. Windflower followed too, a little slower and more discreetly in case Tizzard needed his help. But Tizzard didn't look like he needed any help right now. Cormier had insulted his province and his home town and Tizzard would gladly set Cormier straight if he got out of line.

Being Friday afternoon it wasn't surprising that Cormier couldn't reach his lawyer right away. The lawyer was in St. John's and couldn't likely get here until tomorrow morning anyway. Just as Windflower had planned.

"Put him back in his cell," Windflower told Tizzard.

Cormier was not a happy camper as Tizzard led him back and locked him up for the night. Friday night was probably the best night of the week at the Pink Lady and Cormier hated missing any of the money or the action.

Tizzard found Windflower in his office. "That went well," he said sarcastically to his Sergeant.

"One step at a time, Tizzard," said Windflower. "The lawyer will eventually call back and when he does I want you to tell him that we're holding Cormier as a person of interest in the Elias Martin case. That should get his attention. He can come and see his client anytime he wants. I suspect that won't be until around 11 tomorrow morning since he has to drive in from St. John's and he won't likely give up his Friday social calendar for Cormier. Can you stay here tonight to keep Cormier company?"

"No problem, Boss," said Tizzard. "I guess we'll have to feed him too."

"Yeah, get yourself and him something from the take-out and just put it on your expense claim. I'll stay here until you get back. You can bunk down in the extra cell when you get tired," said Windflower. "I'll pick up some breakfast for all of us in the morning. I'm thinking that Mr. Cormier would like a continental breakfast, don't you? And by the way what did you find out about our friend, Roger Buffet?"

"According to the fellers at the wharf Buffet hasn't had a regular job for a long time," Tizzard said. "Both him and his missus are getting the old age pension and he got a few dollars from the government when he got out of the inshore fishery years ago. He used to work in the lumber yard down at Chester Dawes a few years back but they couldn't risk having a drunk around with the trucks and the forklifts and they had to let him go. Since that time he has been more of a nuisance to everybody else."

"Yeah, I saw his file. He's spent more than a few nights in the back here. I'm thinking that he's not really in any shape to commit anything other than a loud tongue-lashing. What do you think?"

"I agree," said Tizzard, happy to be asked for his opinion. "He may have liked to hurt Elias Martin but I don't think he had the ability to follow through."

"Oh, well, that kinda puts a bit more pressure on us to get something out of Cormier, doesn't it?" said Windflower. "You take good care of him."

Tizzard laughed. "I'm sure me and my new buddy will have a swell sleepover together," he said and he left to pick up the food.

After Tizzard had left, Windflower walked back to Cormier's cell where the prisoner was sulkily pacing the narrow space.

"Youse will never make this stick," he said coldly to the Sergeant.

"Somebody is responsible for Elias Martin's death," said Windflower just as coldly, "and right now you're number one on the hit parade."

He turned and walked away as Cormier launched into another crude and very loud version of his curse word vocabulary. Bilingual too, thought Windflower. That's a nice touch.

Tizzard soon returned with two takeout orders of fried chicken and chips and Windflower said goodnight and headed for home. The sun was just falling into the ocean and the fog had lifted briefly enough for Windflower to enjoy a beautiful pink sunset. Maybe this meant that tomorrow would be a fine day too. He hoped so, especially since he and Sheila were going over to St. Pierre in the evening.

But he had little time to think about tomorrow's activities. He hoped that he had done enough to convince Cormier that they were serious about charging him with murder. More importantly Cormier would have the whole night to consider whether he wanted to go down that road alone.

Chapter Twenty-Eight

Windflower walked over to the taxi stand to make arrangements for a taxi to pick him and Sheila up the next day and instead of going straight home he decided to stop in to visit Howard Stoodley, one of his few friends in Grand Bank, and a retired Crown Attorney. He wanted to say hello to his buddy but he also wanted to pick his brains on the options in front of him.

Howard Stoodley lived in a large brown saltbox house that stood right on the water's edge. At the back of his property was a stone wall and a mesh fence to keep him and his house from being blown out to sea on a stormy night. Since his retirement he had taken up painting seascapes and the ever-changing ocean gave him an endless supply of material.

Windflower found Stoodley in his sun porch studio, brush in hand and a half-finished painting on his easel. "That's pretty good, Howard. I think you're getting better," he said.

"Winston, good to see you. I think that after you paint the same scene a couple of hundred times it's hard not to improve," said Stoodley. "Cuppa?"

"Sure," said Windflower. "I'd also like a few minutes of your time if you can tear yourself away."

"I'm grateful for the break and the company. Moira is off to St. John's to do some shopping and won't be back til Monday. So what's on your mind?" asked Stoodley.

"I'm sorry that this is more than just a social call, Howard. I need your best ex-Crown Attorney's advice, said Windflower.

"I kinda figured that one out," said Stoodley as he poured them both a cup of tea.

After listening to Windflower's story Stoodley sat back for a few minutes and sipped his tea.

"You don't have enough to charge Cormier with murder, even with the other evidence," he said. "His lawyer will know that as soon as you lay it out. But Cormier doesn't. I suggest that you try and talk with Cormier one more time before his lawyer gets here. Totally informally and off the record, of course."

"Tell him you're going to have his bail revoked and charge him with murder. But if he cooperates you are prepared to make him a Crown witness and get him into the witness protection program. You can also tell him that you'll talk to the Crown Attorney about having the assault charge reduced to time served plus a suspended sentence. All he has to do is to tell you who ordered him to do it."

"You can try it out anyway and I'll make some calls to my old colleagues and see if I can't smooth the way. It may not work, but I guarantee you that once his lawyer gets here, Cormier is likely going to walk."

"I can still hold him on the bail violations," said Windflower.

"You would have to transfer him back to Marystown, and I'm assuming there's a reason you don't want to do that," said Stoodley.

"Yeah, MacIntosh," said Windflower. "I heard from someone in St. John's that they had Harvey Brenton on some other matters but the case got dropped just as they were closing in. I'm kind of gun-shy about who I share this with."

"Don't blame you there," said Stoodley. "I've had a few dealings with the Inspector over the years, none of them pleasant. He seemed a little too anxious to please the higher-ups if you know what I mean."

"Thanks for your help, Howard, I really appreciate it," said Windflower. "I'm going to let Cormier have a quiet night in Grand Bank and I'm going to have one as well. I'll talk to him in the morning before his lawyer gets here."

"That's a good plan," said Stoodley. "If I hear anything else I'll give you a call. You know we really should try and get together more often, Winston."

 "Agreed," said Windflower "and I'll try and make my next visit a social call only."

"Why don't you come over next week? Me and Moira are having a few people over for dinner on Thursday. Why don't you bring your lady friend along as well?" asked Stoodley.

When Windflower's eyebrows went up Stoodley just laughed and said "You don't think you could get away with a budding romance in a small town like Grand Bank, did you? You and your lovely café owner are the talk of the town, me boy."

Windflower just smiled and waved goodbye to his friend. So much for keeping my love life a secret, he thought. He had a light snack and settled down on the couch to dig into his book and relax. The next thing he remembered was waking up in the morning.

He recalled taking his book to bed with him and not much more. But he felt more refreshed than he had been for a long time and given the day in front of him he was grateful for at least that.

After his coffee and morning rituals he walked up to the supermarket to get a package of croissants and a large fruit bowl for breakfast. The walk back to the RCMP detachment was a fairly long one by Grand Bank standards but the sun was already bright and shining. A great morning to be alive thought Windflower.

Chapter Twenty-Nine

When he arrived at the detachment Tizzard had already made coffee and Windflower split his croissants and fruit into three portions. "So how was your night?" he asked Tizzard.

"It was pretty quiet," said Tizzard. "Cormier didn't make a peep after you left and other than the shift change it was as dead as a church," said Tizzard.

"Did we hear from Cormier's lawyer?" asked Windflower.

"Donald Delaney will be here around 11 this morning," said Tizzard.

"Bring our guest his breakfast," said Windflower.

Windflower poured himself a cup of coffee and bit into his croissant. A nice peaceful morning until a storm blew into his office in the form of one Harvey Brenton.

"Good morning, Mr. Brenton," said Windflower. "How can we help you this morning?"

"Never mind the bullshit. You've got one of my men in here and I've come to get him out," said Brenton.

"Excuse me Mr. Brenton, but as you can see this is a police station and we decide who to let in and who to let out," said Windflower calmly.

"Do you know who you're talking to? I could have you kicked off the force," snarled Brenton.

"You may think you're powerful out there," said Windflower, pointing out the window, "but in here I call the shots."

"I want to see Cormier," said Brenton. "I know he's in there and in a couple of hours his lawyer will be here to get him out."

"And what is your relationship to Mr. Cormier?" asked Windflower.

"I told you he works for me," said Brenton.

"So you get up early Saturday morning to see all your employees?" asked Windflower.

"Don't be smart with me," said Brenton. "Just let me talk to him before you get yourself into bigger trouble."

"Wait here," said Windflower. "I'll see if he's finished his breakfast."

Windflower went to the back and pulled Tizzard aside. "Harvey Brenton is in the front lobby looking to speak to Cormier. I want you to bring Cormier to the interview room but first I want you to set up the mike and tape recorder."

Tizzard nodded and went to the interview room where he switched on the hidden microphone and recorder. When he had brought Cormier into the room Windflower brought Harvey Brenton back. After they closed the door and left the two men alone Tizzard asked, "Is this legal, Boss?"

"I don't think there's any client-solicitor privilege between an employee and an employer, is there Tizzard? Besides we are just gathering information."

"I guess so," said Tizzard.

"Then shut up and listen," said Windflower.

Through the hidden microphone Windflower and Tizzard could hear Cormier and his boss speaking in very hushed tones but they could still make out most of what the men were talking about.

"Don't say a word to these cops, Cormier, Delaney will be here later this morning to get you out and I'll make it worth your while to stay quiet," they heard Brenton say to Cormier.

"But the big one sez they got me prints at the Martin house and dey are going to charge me with murder," replied Cormier.

"They're just trying to scare you," said Brenton. "Unless you squeal they don't have anything on you and if you know what's good for you you'll keep that big trap shut. I'm telling you don't worry. They don't have enough to charge you or they would have done that already. Now sit tight and don't say another word til Delaney gets here. Ok?"

Windflower couldn't see it but Cormier nodded his okay to Harvey Brenton. Soon Brenton was yelling loudly to get out.

"Everything satisfactory, Mr. Brenton?" asked Windflower.

"He'll be out in two hours, as soon as his lawyer gets here. You have nothing to hold him on," said Brenton.

"That's what he says," said Windflower. "Once we get a little more evidence we'll see what a judge has to say about that." It was a bit of bravado but Windflower just couldn't resist.

"You still don't know who you're dealing with do you?" asked Brenton. "You'll soon be sorry you pulled this stunt."

"Have a nice day, Mr. Brenton," said Windflower to Harvey Brenton's back as the other man sped out of the office and peeled out of the parking lot.

"So what do you think, Sarge?" asked Tizzard as he came up front after re-locking Cormier in his cell.

"I think we now know for sure that Harvey Brenton was involved and we also know how difficult this will be to prove. Our only chance is to get Cormier to roll over on Harvey Brenton. That won't be easy since I think he's very afraid of his boss."

"I agree," said Tizzard. "I guess we'll have to find a way to make him more afraid of us or make him a better offer."

"My thinking exactly Constable. You know you may be Sergeant material after all, Tizzard," said Windflower.

"Really?" said Tizzard, more than a little pleased.

"I mean it Tizzard. If somehow we manage to crack this case I'm going to make a recommendation on your promotion to Corporal. Of course if it goes the other way, I may be needing your help."

"No problem, Boss. I got your back either way," said Tizzard.

"Okay, I guess it's time to see if my music can calm the savage beast. Wish me luck, Tizzard. Let me know if the lawyer arrives," he said.

Windflower took a deep breath and wandered to the back cell where Cormier was lying on his back, his eyes closed.

"Is my lawyer here yet?" Cormier asked.

"Not yet," said Windflower, "but I wanted to talk to you first before he got here."

"I got nuttin to say," said Cormier.

"All you got to do is listen," said Windflower.

Cormier scowled but nodded.

"We know that you didn't plan this thing on your own," Windflower began. "We know that Harvey Brenton put you up to this but unless you speak up now, the train is going down the tracks and you will be the only one charged for murder. And I'll guarantee that there's no bail so that will mean a minimum of a year waiting for trial plus another 20 to 25 afterwards. Plus whatever you get on the assault charge.

I hear that the Marystown guys are looking at having the charges increased because of your record. So here's what I can do for you."

Chapter Thirty

"Are you offering me a deal?" asked Cormier.

"If you testify about Harvey Brenton we will waive the murder charge and I'll see what I can do about getting the assault charge reduced so that your sentence will be suspended."

"Harvey Brenton will kill me if I testifies against im," said Cormier, suddenly honest and forgetting his vow of silence.

"We can get you into a witness protection program in Quebec far away from Harvey Brenton. You'll be in a safe house somewhere in Montreal until the trial," answered Windflower.

Windflower paused and waited to see if there was any reaction from Cormier.

"Would there be a reward too?" Cormier finally asked.

"You did help kill Elias Martin," said Windflower. "I don't think we can reward you for that, but there is some expense money in the program and I suspect you have a few dollars put aside to keep you going."

"I'll think about it," said Cormier. "But first I wants to see what my lawyer sez about getting me out of here."

Windflower went back to the front office and joined Tizzard. About an hour later a sleek Lincoln Town Car pulled up in front of them. "That would be our lawyer," said Windflower.

The man who stepped out of the car had silver-white hair that was kind of spiked on top to show that he was up on the latest style. He wore a light blue sweater over a crisp white shirt and impeccably creased baby blue pants. His sunglasses and shoes could have probably covered a week of Tizzard's salary. Impressive, thought Windflower.

"Good morning," the lawyer said. "My name is Donald Delaney and I'm here to see my client, Patrick Cormier. What are the charges against him?"

"Good morning, Mr. Delaney," said Windflower. "I'm Sergeant Windflower and this is Constable Tizzard. There are no charges against Mr. Cormier, but we are holding him as a person of interest in a murder case."

"I'll see my client now," said Delaney.

"Constable, please take Mr. Delaney to the interview room and bring Mr. Cormier to see him."

"Thank you Sergeant," said the lawyer.

After about fifteen minutes Windflower and Tizzard heard Delaney calling out to them. "You stay here and I'll go see what he wants," said Windflower.

Windflower went to the interview room and sat across from Delaney who was sitting next to his client.

"Unless you are prepared to charge Mr. Cormier now I suggest you let him go," said Delaney. "Your evidence is flimsy and nothing ties my client directly to any event or action concerning the late Mr. Martin."

"What about the fingerprints?" asked Windflower?

Delaney paused and smiled at Windflower. "You may or may not have Mr. Cormier's fingerprints on some object in or near Mr. Martin's house but you have no way to prove whether these fingerprints were placed on these objects by Mr. Cormier before or after they arrived at Mr. Martin's house. Mr. Cormier has no known contact with Mr. Martin and you have no evidence to even place him in Grand Bank for the last six months. You simply don't have enough to charge Mr. Cormier. Unless you want to face false arrest charges yourself Sergeant, I strongly suggest you let him go."

By this point Cormier was grinning broadly. Windflower knew it was useless to proceed down this avenue any further. So he decided to pursue his other line of attack.

"There's still the matter of the bail violations," said Windflower. "You should know about them since you signed the bail application yourself."

"I'm sure that's all a misunderstanding, Sergeant but it's also out of your jurisdiction. I am requesting that Mr. Cormier be transferred back to Marystown without delay and I assure you that as soon as I or one of my colleagues can get this matter in front of a judge, Mr. Cormier will be released," said Delaney.

"Very well," said Windflower, realizing when he had been beaten. "I will ask Constable Tizzard to drive Mr. Cormier back to Marystown this afternoon."

"Thank you Sergeant and have a good day," said Delaney and he marched out of the interview room and into his Lincoln, another easy $1000 in his pockets.

"Just like I taut," said Cormier. "Youse got nuttin on me."

Windflower called Tizzard and told him to put Cormier back in his cell.

"Hey, youse gotta take me back to Marystown," yelled Cormier.

Windflower ignored him and went back up front. When Tizzard came out he told him the bad news. "You've got to take him back to Marystown. Delaney was right. We don't have enough to charge him or even hold him. Wait an hour or so and then take him back."

"Shoot," said Tizzard. "Sorry, Sarge. It's just that we know he's our only link to Harvey Brenton."

"After you're finished with that, take the rest of the weekend off. You deserve it," said Windflower.

"How about you, Boss, got any big plans for the weekend?" asked Tizzard.

"Actually I do," said Windflower.

Chapter Thirty-One

Windflower walked home feeling tired and dejected. At least he had his evening in St. Pierre to look forward to. He lounged around his house for a few hours until it was time to get ready. A hot shower, a smooth shave and a dash of aftershave woke him up. He put on a crisp, clean white shirt and dark blue dress pants to go with his new navy blue blazer. No tie but a beautiful baby blue silk handkerchief in his lapel made him feel like a real human again.

Just before 4 he walked over to Sheila's with a whistle on his lips and a definite stride in his step. Sheila looked stunning when she opened the door. She had her long red hair up with tiny ringlets dangling down the sides. She wore a dazzling white dress that came to just above her knees, a crimson red angora shawl over her shoulders and black strapless spiked heels. A single strand of pearls completed her look.

"You look amazing," said Windflower

"You look pretty dashing yourself," said Sheila.

"I bet the neighbours would love to see us like this," said Windflower.

"Don't worry," said Sheila, "they're all peeking out their windows right now."

"Howard Stoodley told me that we are the talk of the town," said Windflower.

"Does that bother you?" asked Sheila.

"Not in the least," said Windflower. "Here's our ride."

On the short ride to Fortune the couple shared pleasantries about their good fortune at having a fine day for their boat ride and excursion to St. Pierre. When they arrived at the dock the RCMP cruiser was waiting for them. Windflower exchanged greetings with his old buddy the skipper and introduced Sheila. Sheila was escorted inside by Windflower and the skipper and they were soon underway. Windflower went up on deck with the skipper for a few minutes but was soon back inside with his date.

"I love seeing Grand Bank from this side of the water," said Sheila peering out through the cruiser's cabin. "My grandfather used to take me out here sometimes in his dory when the weather was calm. I used to always imagine that I was an explorer who'd just discovered a new land."

"It sure is a beautiful sight," said Windflower. I haven't been out here too much, just on a few smuggling patrols, but I can almost picture Grand Bank when it was the home of the ship building industry in this part of the world. I heard once that there were up to seven Grand Bank schooners being built here at a time."

"Yes and the full waterfront was laid out with cod fish being unloaded, cleaned or drying on the flakes. I don't remember those days myself," she laughed, "but I have seen the pictures."

The couple sat closely together on the boat and when Windflower reached out for Sheila's hand she gladly clasped it. After about 45 minutes the dock of St. Pierre loomed closer.

"Do you know the history of St. Pierre?" asked Sheila.

"I know it's reputation as a great outlet for South Coast liquor smugglers," said Windflower.

"That's true enough," said Sheila, "but there's quite a bit more to know about St. Pierre and its sister island of Miquelon." She went on to tell Windflower that the islands were part of a small archipelago off the south coast of Newfoundland that were first discovered by the Portuguese and then claimed by Jacques Cartier for the French on his second voyage to the St. Lawrence River colonies. France lost claim to the islands after the Seven Years War but their sovereignty was returned to France by the Treaty of Paris in 1763.

Over the years there were numerous fights over their ownership with the fishermen from Newfoundland but in 1815 the island came into French hands permanently. Its biggest claim to fame was as an offshore base where the Canadian distillers warehoused huge stocks of Canadian whiskey during prohibition. At one time in the 1930's there were up to 300,000 cases of whiskey per month illegally shipped to the States from St. Pierre.

"I told you they were famous for smuggling liquor," said Windflower. "But I'm very happy to be with a beautiful and intelligent woman like you to hear about it first hand."

Sheila just laughed as both she and Windflower felt the boat nudge up against the wharf in St. Pierre. After a brief thank you and goodbye to the skipper they were soon on land again, although this time in another country, France. They proceeded smoothly through customs and were soon walking along the main street of the tiny island.

They browsed through the small shops that featured French and European perfumes, clothing and jewelry along with numerous stores that sold an endless variety of liquors and cigarettes. They didn't find anything they really wanted to buy but were just happy to hang around together.

"It's always amazing to me that even though we share the same waters and weather that things are so different over here," said Sheila.

"It is different," said Windflower noticing the Peugeots and Renaults lining the streets," but with the exception of better fashion sense for the ladies, present company excepted, this could just as easy be another Newfoundland outport. And the language, of course."

"I suppose you're right," said Sheila. "They're mostly just fishermen trying to make a living."

"How about a coffee?" asked Windflower.

"Perfect," said Sheila.

They stopped at a small café and had large white bowls of café au lait while they gazed out at the water. Almost before they knew it the sun was gone down and it was time for dinner.

They walked over to the restaurant that had been recommended to Windflower. La Voilerie was in a perfect location, right on the water. They were shown to their table by a surly French waiter but their good mood would not be shattered by any of his arrogance. They ordered the prix fixe menu and a litre of the house red. Their dinner was long, delicious and provided an opportunity for them to finally start sharing their feelings with each other.

Over escargots in a garlicky butter sauce Sheila talked about her late husband and Windflower about his former fiancé. Their salade niçoise with cucumbers, red peppers, tomatoes, onions, hard boiled eggs, anchovies and black olives allowed them time to talk about the challenges of being a police officer and running a café. With their plateau de fruits de mer that featured oysters, clams, shrimp, salmon, and mussels in a tangy tomato broth they talked about what they would like to do in the future. Sheila wanted to travel more and finally have children before it was too late. Windflower liked both these ideas, especially travel to somewhere where it was warm and sunny all the time.

By the time their dessert had arrived they were happy just to savour the deep rich taste of the chocolate molten lava cake and sip their coffees.

"That was the best meal I have had in a long time," said Sheila. "And I didn't have to cook or clean up."

"I'm glad you enjoyed it," said Windflower. "I wouldn't want to eat like that every night. I'd be over 300 pounds."

They strolled out into the night which had certainly grown chillier since the afternoon. Sheila wrapped her shawl around her tightly and Windflower put his arm around her protectively. She snuggled in close to him as they walked together to the dock where the RCMP cruiser was tied up. Saying hello to the skipper they got on board and went immediately to the cabin to get warm.

An hour later they were back in Fortune where their cab was waiting to take them home. Windflower walked Sheila to her door and she invited him in for a nightcap. He made himself comfortable while she put on the kettle and got out a bottle of brandy and two snifters. Soon they were sitting quietly on the coach with Windflower's arm around her.

"Winston," said Sheila, "I think we have the opportunity to have something really special together. I really care about you and think you're a wonderful man."

"I really care for you too," said Windflower.

"But I am worried that we will start into something and you will be transferred out of here. I am not sure that I want to leave Grand Bank and I sure don't want to be traipsing all over the country after you," said Sheila.

"I've thought about that too," said Windflower, thinking about Anne-Marie and her decision to go her own way rather than blindly following along his career path. "After 10 years on the force you can apply for an extended stay in a position," he added, "and I'm thinking about doing that to stay in Grand Bank."

"Oh, Winston, that would be great," said Sheila wrapping her arms around him and kissing him deeply.

"That was nice," said Windflower, returning her kiss with equal fervour. "I hope there's more where that came from."

"There sure is, but not tonight," laughed Sheila. "I've got the early shift at the café tomorrow morning."

"I'll let you get to bed, then," said Windflower. "I'll drop over later in the morning to see you. I guess we're an item now, Sheila. Are we going steady?"

"I guess we are," said Sheila and gave him another deep kiss as he left for home.

I think I'm in love, thought Windflower.

Chapter Thirty-Two

Windflower woke early Sunday morning without needing the alarm to remind him. He liked Sundays, the quiet and peacefulness that surrounded it, even with Sunday shopping. He got up to see the sun was already shining brightly, not a cloud or a fog bank in sight. Maybe this was finally spring he thought, although in Newfoundland spring was usually limited to a few days in May, and that was always iffy. Better to just enjoy the day than hope for a season.

He took his time doing his morning smudge and prayers and laid out tobacco to allow for a better connection with the Creator and to be open to the universe. As his spirit awakened he felt an overwhelming sense of gratitude and love. He immediately gave thanks for the wonderful woman who was going to be a bigger part of his life.

Windflower went back inside and turned on the coffee, made himself some scrambled eggs and toast and got his book from the bedroom. He usually read and re-read great literature like Eliot, Chaucer, and Shakespeare, adding in Dickens for pure enjoyment. But now he was reading a modern book, Joseph Boyden's "Three Day Road" about two young Indians who were trying to survive as Canadian soldiers in the midst of the First World War. After cleaning up from breakfast he was off to his other Sunday morning routine, doing his laundry.

He picked up his laundry bag and walked over to the Laundromat. It was always quiet here on Sunday morning and he spent an enjoyable couple of hours while his clothes washed and dried themselves. A few minutes of folding and he was on his way.

When he got back home he checked his cell phone for messages and there were two. The first was from Sheila thanking him for a lovely evening and the other was from Bill Genges in St. John's. He would see Sheila later. He wanted to know what Genges had found out.

"Good morning, Genges here," a voice answered.

"Bill, it's Winston Windflower. What have you got for me?" he asked.

"It's arsenic all right. In every container we checked. I'm no expert but what we found is certainly enough to kill somebody if applied regularly over a period of time," said Genges.

"Thanks, Bill, that is good news," said Windflower.

"So how did you make out with the other guy, Cormier?" asked Genges.

"We found him in Marystown but so far he's not cooperating," said Windflower.

"Too bad. Well good luck on the case," said Genges. "If you need anything else just let me know."

"Thanks again Bill," said Windflower as he hung up.

Well at least we have confirmation on the means, thought Windflower. Not that it's likely to do us any good. Might as well go by and see Sheila and have another cup of coffee.

As Windflower was leaving his house his cell phone rang again. "Windflower," he answered.

"Sarge, it's Tizzard. I dropped Cormier at the Marystown lockup last night so the locals could check into his bail violations but I just got a call from my buddy there. Cormier was stabbed early this morning in the Marystown jail and he's in hospital getting sewn up!!"

"What the hell happened over there?" asked Windflower.

"Apparently they let all the guys in the jail out for an hour or so in the yard to get some fresh air and while Cormier was out someone stuck a home-made shiv in his back. He lost a lot of blood and he's in serious but stable condition in the Marystown hospital, said Tizzard."

"Wow!" said Windflower, "that didn't take long. Do they have any idea who did it?"

"Well it was clearly one of his jail mates but the guards on duty reported a fight in the yard and couldn't see who did it. By the time they got outside there was blood over most of them. It could be anyone of them. They do an investigation but my buddy figures they'll never pin this on anybody," said Tizzard. "I think Harvey Brenton is involved."

"I think so too," said Windflower. "I bet the lawyer tipped him off where Cormier was going to be last night. But once again we have absolutely no proof. I'm getting a little tired of this scenario."

"Me too," said Tizzard. "So what are we going to do?"

"We aren't going to do anything," said Windflower. "You are going to enjoy your day off but I am going to take a ride over to Marystown later on to see if I can talk to Cormier. Maybe he'll be in more of a mood to listen now. Do you think you can call your buddy in Marystown and clear this with them?"

"Sure thing, Boss," said Tizzard. "I'll call you back."

Another blatant criminal act that had Harvey Brenton written all over it but unlikely to ever be prosecuted, thought Windflower. This is really starting to piss me off.

To clear his head and his mood Windflower decided to go back to his original plan of seeing Sheila and getting a cup of coffee at the Mug-Up. The café was bustling when he entered, people coming and going from church and sundry other Sunday morning activities. He waved to Sheila at the counter and found his usual spot in the corner. Sheila was busy serving customers for a few minutes but as soon as she could she dropped over to Windflower's table.

"Thank you for my nice message," said Windflower. "I thought I'd give you my reply in person."

"That's very nice Winston," Sheila beamed. "I had a great time."

"I was wondering if you'd like to come on another date with me," said Windflower. "Howard invited me for dinner at his place on Thursday and I'd love to have you come with me. It could be like our coming-out party."

"That would be great," said Sheila. "I'm a little busy this morning but maybe we can get together later this evening."

"I'd like to, but I have to go to Marystown this evening," said Windflower.

"Got some shopping to do at Wal-Mart?" she teased, knowing the way Windflower hated the impact that big-box stores had on local communities.

"No way," said Windflower, then realizing she was just kidding, he added, "just a little police business."

"Well, good luck with that. Coffee or tea?" she asked.

"Coffee please, Sheila," he replied.

Chapter Thirty-Three

As Windflower sipped his coffee he watched as the good people of Grand Bank innocently went about their Sunday morning. They had little idea what was going on behind their backs but Windflower did and he also knew that it was up to him to do something about it.

On his way home Tizzard called to let him know that the officer who was guarding Cormier's room at the Marystown hospital was aware that he might be coming to visit. Windflower thanked Tizzard and instead of continuing home decided to drop in again on Howard Stoodley.

This time when he went to Stoodley's back door he was not in his sun porch gallery. Windflower found him in the kitchen on the phone. Stoodley waved hello and gestured for Windflower to take a seat while he continued his phone conversation.

"That's great Herb. Thanks for the info. If you're ever out this way drop in and I'll give you a sketch in payment." Stoodley laughed at his friend's response, said goodbye and hung up the phone.

"Morning, Winston. I've just been doing my legwork like you asked. It's fun to be back in the game again, well at least for a couple of days," he said.

"That's good," said Windflower. "I'm here for info and advice as usual, but I also wanted to accept your invitation to dinner on Thursday and Sheila is coming with me, if that's okay."

"That's terrific, Winston," said Stoodley. "We're cooking up a Jiggs Dinner; salt meat, cabbage, pease pudding, the works.

Actually Moira is doing most of the cooking. I'll probably be chief potato peeler."

"So you're finally going to let the genie out of the bottle?" Stoodley continued. "It must be serious."

"We'll see," was all Windflower would reply to that speculation. "So I should bring you up to speed." Windflower then ran through his conversations with Harvey Brenton, Cormier and the lawyer and told Stoodley about the stabbing.

"It's Harvey Brenton, isn't it?" Stoodley asked, more of a statement than a question.

"I'm pretty sure," said Windflower. "Delaney would have told him that Cormier was back in Marystown and Brenton just put the word out to send Cormier a message, if not to kill him. The more I know about Brenton, the more I realize how dangerous and slippery he is."

"I know," said Stoodley. "That guy I just talked to was Herb Cranston, one of the finest Crown Attorneys you'll ever meet. He was on a case involving drugs and money laundering that was linked to Harvey Brenton before it got squashed."

"I heard about that case from a guy in Commercial Crime," said Windflower. "So where did the order to stop the investigation come from?" he asked.

"Right from the Minister's office," said Stoodley, "on the advice of a senior RCMP officer."

"MacIntosh," said Windflower.

"Probably," said Stoodley. "You know maybe there's a way to pull all these cases together. You don't care who gets the credit for this, do you Winston?"

"Not a bit," said Windflower. "The only thing I really want is to get Harvey Brenton put away and if there's a way to get MacIntosh out of this area that would be a bonus."

"Here's my thinking then. We might be able to get the drug case re-opened if you can somehow find a way to get Cormier to cooperate," said Stoodley.

"I'm going over to see him in the hospital this evening," said Windflower. "The carrot didn't work so well, but maybe the stick from Harvey Brenton might be a way to convince Mr. Cormier that we are his only way out."

"Okay," said Stoodley. "I'm going to call Herb back and tell him the latest. If you can get Cormier to play along we'll have to move quickly so he'll have to talk to the drug guys to tell them what's up."

"Agreed," said Windflower. "I'll call you when I have some news. One more thing Howard, even if the drug guys take over I still want Harvey Brenton charged with Elias Martin's death. We at least owe his family that."

"I'll see what I can do," said Stoodley.

As Windflower left Howard Stoodley's house he noticed the eternal fog was once again sliding in slowly over the water dropping the temperature at least 5 degrees. I guess spring is over he thought.

Windflower went home and tried to relax but even his book couldn't get him to sit still. So he went into his bedroom and changed into his RCMP uniform. He wanted his visit to Patrick Cormier to look and feel completely official. If he was going down he wanted to do it with his RCMP boots on. He walked back to the detachment to pick up his vehicle through a now completely dense cover of fog. Better to head out early on a day like this. At dusk or in the nighttime the ever present moose had a tendency to appear on the highway without any warning.

Windflower had already had his share of close calls with these massive animals and knew better than most that a car had little chance against these thousand pound plus mammals. They may be as dumb as cows but many times they just crush a vehicle and its passengers and walk away unharmed.

Soon he was on the highway to Marystown, crossing the barren rugged land with scarcely a soul or another vehicle for company. As he neared Marystown the traffic picked up, many of the cars heading for his despised Wal-Mart and the rest to Tim Hortons.

Windflower decided to stop at Tim Hortons himself for a large coffee; double-double, and a maple dip donut. He really didn't need the coffee and the donut was hardly the lunch he should be eating but he wanted a few moments to relax and compose himself before he got to the hospital.

Chapter Thirty-Four

Windflower finished his coffee and donut and realized that he couldn't put off the visit to the hospital any longer. He parked his patrol car in front of the Marystown Hospital near the Emergency Exit and went inside. At reception he was directed to a secure ward on the 3rd floor. Windflower had been there one time before with a totally psychotic teenager who had overdosed on some variation of ecstasy that someone had shipped back to Grand Bank from St. John's.

When he got to the ward he rang the buzzer and a male orderly saw his uniform and let him in. "Room 319," the orderly said, "Down the hall and turn left."

Windflower turned the corner and saw an RCMP constable sitting on a chair outside the room. When the constable saw Windflower he jumped to his feet.

"I'm Windflower," he said.

"I'm McGuire," the constable replied. "I got word you were coming."

"How is he?" asked Windflower.

"He's a bit groggy. They've got him hooked up to a morphine drip that kicks in every two hours. But he's going to make it. You can't easily kill a snake like that," said McGuire.

"You keep watch out here," said Windflower, "and don't let anyone----nurses, doctors, anyone in until I come out, okay?"

"Okay Sergeant," said McGuire.

Windflower went into Cormier's room which was dark except for a light over the I.V. drip. The morphine, thought Windflower.

Cormier was lying on his stomach with a bed sheet that covered his legs and buttocks. There was a thick white bandage wrapped tightly around his upper back. Windflower sat in a chair next to his bed and watched Cormier drift in and out of sleep. He could tell by Cormier's breathing and the twitching in his legs that it was about time for the morphine to kick in. He silently reached over and flipped the switch to off. He needed Cormier awake and attentive to talk to him, more importantly to get him to listen. After a few minutes Cormier started to moan and wake up.

"Good evening, Mr. Cormier, remember me?" Windflower asked.

Cormier opened one eye, groaned and started reciting his extensive vocabulary of oaths and curses. Windflower listened for a while and finally said, "I've turned off your pain killers, Cormier. The faster you and I have our chat, the faster you can have your morphine back."

Another string of profanities followed but finally Cormier said, "What do you want?"

"Since you refused my earlier offer I thought I'd give you a chance to reconsider," said Windflower, "but now the stakes are much higher, for me and for you."

Windflower paused until he was sure he had Cormier's attention and then he continued. "First of all Harvey Brenton tried to have you killed in the Marystown jail. You know it and I know it. Your friend, the lawyer, must have told him where you'd be. I'm just surprised they didn't finish the job. What Harvey Brenton wants he usually gets, doesn't he Mr. Cormier? If he wants you dead it can happen anytime, anywhere. Maybe even in this hospital room."

"Secondly, we're no longer talking about the murder of an old man. Now we want the full goods. The drugs, the money-laundering, the cigarette smuggling. We want to know about your role in these operations and what Harvey Brenton asked you to do. Are you with me so far?" asked Windflower.

"Turn on the god damn morphine," said Cormier.

"Not until we reach some understanding," said Windflower. "So here's the deal. You tell us everything you know about Brenton's operation and we give you full immunity and witness protection and relocation. We bring the drug guys in tonight and they take over the case and your custody. Or you can take your chances with Harvey Brenton. What do you say Mr. Cormier?"

"I don't have much choice, do I?" asked Cormier.

"Not if you want to stay alive," said Windflower.

"Ok, Ok, now turn on the frigging morphine," squealed Cormier.

"No problem," said Windflower flicking the switch back to the on position and watching Cormier's face relax in relief.

"Screw me on this and I'll get you," said Windflower. "One more thing I want a statement from you about what happened to Elias Martin. Agreed?"

"Yes," said Cormier who felt well enough to unleash another barrage of vulgarities at Windflower's back as he left the room.

"Thank you, Constable," said Windflower as he went back out into the hall. "I have to make a phone call and then I'll be back. It appears that Mr. Cormier may just have a few more visitors tonight."

Windflower went outside and phoned Howard Stoodley. "It's a go," he said. "Cormier is ready to roll over on Harvey Brenton but things will have to happen tonight. I'm not sure we can keep Cormier safe even in here and we don't want to give him any time to change his mind."

"I've already talked to Herb and he's got the drug squad ready to roll as soon as they get the word. They have a helicopter on stand by and can be there in an hour once we give them the green light. I'll call Herb right now and give him the good news."

Windflower got two coffees out of the drink dispenser and went back up to the third floor. He gave McGuire one of the coffees and got a chair for himself to join the vigil on Cormier. About 10 minutes later his phone rang. It was Stoodley telling him that the drug guys were enroute to Marystown from St. John's to take over the prisoner.

"MacIntosh won't be too happy about this," said Windflower.

"MacIntosh has been ordered back to St. John's for an interview," replied Stoodley. "They may not be able to nail him with anything specific but they will get him out of the way. After last time they're not taking any chances."

True to Stoodley's promise about an hour later three heavily armed members of the RCMP drug squad came into the area where McGuire and Windflower were sitting.

"You can go home, Constable," said the lead guy. "We'll take over from here."

After McGuire left he turned to Windflower and said "I'm Pomeroy with the drug squad. Thank you Sergeant, without your help we couldn't have made any of this happen."

"No problem," said Windflower. "I just hope you get the big guy too."

"I think we will," said Pomeroy. "We'll look after Cormier. Why don't you go home and get some sleep? Maybe tomorrow morning you could come back and we could do a de-brief."

"No problem," said Windflower groggily as he suddenly started to feel the tiredness his body had been experiencing for hours.

That night on the way home to Grand Bank through the treacherous, foggy moose-infested highway, Windflower drove slowly but felt no fear. He gave thanks to the Creator for helping him on his journey and to his ancestors who had clearly been with him. Windflower knew he would sleep like a baby tonight.

Chapter Thirty-Five

The next morning was a bit of a blur. A quick shower, a call to Sheila to give her an update and then back on the road to Marystown. At least a nice sunny day for the ride and Windflower enjoyed the splendid beauty of the wilderness around him until he saw the vast openness of water that was the deep port of Marystown. The shipping below him was busy with the latest project, a sub-contract to build some of the Navy vessels that would bring a brief respite of economic god fortunes to the region.

He parked near the detachment building and walked to the front door. Just as he was opening the door a man burdened down with boxes hurtled towards him. Windflower's first reaction was to offer assistance but when he saw who it was he had second thoughts.

"Windflower," snarled MacIntosh seeming a little surprised and a bit more upset. "I'll be back, don't think I won't," he hissed at Windflower as he pushed his way past.

Windflower didn't say a word but spent a couple of quiet moments watching a suddenly clumsy RCMP Inspector load a few boxes into his car. He may be back, but not if there's anything I can do about it, thought Windflower.

He asked directions from the reception desk and made his way to a small boardroom where Pomeroy and three other officers from the drug squad were drinking coffee and waiting for him.

"Good morning, Windflower," said Pomeroy. "Get yourself a coffee and a muffin."

"Thanks," said Windflower, "don't mind if I do."

"This is Riggs, and Frost and Pacquette," said Pomeroy.

"Good to meet you," said Windflower to all three as he shook their hands. He grabbed a coffee and a muffin and sat at the table.

"So why don't you tell us everything that you know about Cormier and our mutual friend Harvey Brenton. And take your time, we've got all day," said Pomeroy.

"I guess you guys probably know a lot more about Cormier, and Harvey Brenton, for that matter, than I do," said Windflower. "We got Cormier's name after his prints were found on water containers at Elias Martin's house. Those water containers had been tampered with to allow for arsenic to be placed in them and that's how we figured that Elias Martin got poisoned."

"Cormier is a tough nut," continued Windflower. "Not bright, but very tough. He is also very self-interested and as long as he thinks he will be looked after, he'll be fine. He didn't really want to cooperate at the beginning but I managed to get his attention," he concluded.

The other men in the room laughed. "That young constable said that you could hear Cormier yelling the full length of the ward," said Pomeroy. "What did you do?"

"I just asked Mr. Cormier to focus very closely on his own self interest," said Windflower with a smile. "That seemed to work quite well. If you have any problems with Cormier just tell him that I'm going back. That should help mellow him out."

All the drug squad members laughed again at this and Pomeroy said "We'll certainly do that, Sergeant. But I think we can handle Cormier. Tell us what you know about Harvey Brenton."

"Harvey Brenton is not a nice man, which you probably already know, but he really is a mean and probably cruel man as well. There's some suggestion of domestic violence although he's never been charged and a lot of people in the Grand Bank area appear to be afraid of him. But he has not been as successful in business without also looking after the people that work for him and I mean that both ways."

"You think that Brenton had Cormier knifed?" asked Pomeroy.

"Yes," said Windflower. "Cormier's lawyer was the only one who knew that he was being taken back to Marystown and he happens to be Brenton's mouthpiece as well. Even more convincing is the fact that Cormier believes that Brenton was behind it. That's why he decided to roll over on him."

"Interesting, how our Mr. Brenton operates," said Pomeroy. "Anything else?"

"Well, I don't think that he is above paying off anybody who might interfere with his business interests," said Windflower.

"You mean MacIntosh?" asked Pomeroy.

"Not just him. I think that there might be a few other people in the justice and political systems who might be on Harvey Brenton's payroll," said Windflower. "Harvey Brenton is a very smart person and he has not survived and prospered for so long without knowing who's hand to grease along the way."

"Yeah, we've thought the same way for a long time," said Pomeroy. "We've had the noose around Brenton's neck a few times but he's managed to slip away every time. At least MacIntosh will be out of the way this time around."

"I saw the Inspector on the way in," said Windflower. "He did not look happy at all."

"Good," said Pomeroy. "He's been nothing but a pain in the butt since we started working this case. So not having him here will be a relief. "

"So how are you going to set this case up" asked Windflower?

"Glad you asked," said Pomeroy. "First off we are going to pump Cormier for all he's worth. Riggs here has worked with Cormier before. He knows how to, ahem, get his attention as well."

Riggs and his colleagues laughed again and Riggs piped in "But if we want an expert interrogator, we'll call you in Windflower." Everyone including Windflower laughed at this as well.

"I know that you are going to be focusing on the drug side of the story, but we need Cormier to give us the goods on the Elias Martin case as well," said Windflower.

"Good point," said Pomeroy. "In fact that's where we're going to start. We want to use the Elias Martin case to put heat on Brenton. So once we get the story from Cormier we want you to pick up Harvey Brenton and charge him with murder. Maybe we can then leverage this to get him to talk about his drug connections and we can blow this case completely wide open."

"Great," said Windflower. "I don't care what he goes to jail for, as long as he goes to jail. For a very long time."

"Agreed," said Pomeroy. "So we're all on the same page. Riggs is going over to see Cormier this afternoon and assuming that everything goes well you can pick up Harvey Brenton tomorrow morning. How does that sound?"

"That sounds great," said Windflower as he stood to shake hands all around. "I'll be waiting for your call."

The drive home to Grand Bank was one of the few moments for a long time that Windflower had felt relaxed; even serene. This looked like it was going to work out quite well, he thought.

Chapter Thirty-Six

Windflower was gliding along the highway on his way back to Grand Bank when his cell phone rang. He pulled over to the side of the road and turned on his emergency flashers.

"Windflower," he answered.

"Good day, Sergeant, it's Betsy."

"Good day, Betsy," said Windflower, "and how are you this fine Monday?"

"Someone is in a good mood," said Betsy. "I'm very well thank you. Sorry to bother you but Constable Tizzard has been in my office six times to ask if I'd heard from you and if you were coming into the office. He said he heard some good news about your case from Marystown and wanted to talk to you about it. I tried to put him off, but he is persistent."

"He is that," laughed Windflower. "Tell Tizzard that I'm on my way back to Grand Bank right now and to meet me at the Mug-Up in about twenty minutes. Oh, and Betsy, will you start the paperwork for a recommendation to Corporal for Constable Tizzard? I'll fill in my part when I get back into the office. And please keep this quiet. I especially don't want him to know about it in advance."

"No problem," said Betsy. "So I assume that he was right about the good news."

"Yes," said Windflower. "Things are falling into place. Was anybody else looking for me?"

"The Mayor called," said Betsy. "Apparently the patrol picked up his nephew as part of the teenage sweep on the weekend, and he wants to talk to you about it."

"I expect he does," said Windflower. "Anybody else?"

"Oh, yeah," said Betsy. "Howard Stoodley called and left a message for you to call him. He said he had some information for you about an investigation that has been started in the Provincial Department of Justice."

"Thanks, Betsy," said Windflower. "I'll call Howard back. If the Mayor calls again tell him I'm dealing with a murder investigation and I'll get back to him as soon as I can. I should be at the office in about an hour. I'll see you then."

"Okay, Sergeant," said Betsy as she hung up.

Time for some coffee, thought Windflower as he came over the crest of a hill overlooking Grand Bank on a beautifully clear sunny day with only a few scattered whitecaps to threaten its peace. And of course a drug-dealing murderer, thought Windflower.

Windflower pulled his car up close to the entrance to the café, parked and locked his vehicle. He stepped into the heat and good humour of the Mug-Up where people seemed genuinely happy and in good spirits, even for a Monday. Sheila certainly was, and she gave Windflower a bright smile and a friendly wave. Windflower smiled back and tipped his hand to signify that he'd like a coffee. She nodded and went to get him a cup.

"Good day, beautiful lady," said Windflower as Sheila approached with his mug of coffee.

"Hello to you too, Winston," Sheila replied. "How did things go in Marystown?"

"Great," said Windflower. "If everything goes according to plan we should have an arrest very soon."

"That is great news," said Sheila. "But I wonder how she'll take it," she added, pointing to Marge Brenton sitting at a table in the corner of the café.

"Who's that with her?" asked Windflower.

"That's Georgette Sheridan's son," said Sheila. "I guess he stayed around a few days after the funeral to visit."

"Interesting," said Windflower. "I guess I should drop by to say hello. Excuse me Sheila."

Windflower walked over to the table where Marge Brenton was sitting and she noticed him coming first. Windflower thought he saw her ducking a little when he approached as if she was hiding something. As he got nearer he could see what it was. Her face was heavily made up but Windflower could notice tell-tale bruising on her cheek and around her left eye.

"Hello, Mrs. Brenton," he said. "And it's James, isn't it?" he asked the young man.

"Good day Sergeant," replied Marge Brenton and the young man jumped to his feet to offer his hand to Windflower.

"Yes, it's James, James Sheridan," he said quickly.

"How are you today, Mrs. Brenton?" asked Windflower.

"I'm fine, Sergeant," said Marge Brenton.

"If I can ever be of assistance you can certainly call on me," said Windflower, a little boldly, but given the circumstances he felt he should at least offer.

"I know where to find the RCMP," she answered coldly.

"So, have you had any success in finding my uncle's killer?" asked James Sheridan.

Still looking at Marge Brenton, Windflower answered "I think we're making progress and may have an arrest soon."

Marge Brenton simply gazed stonily and did not react. James Sheridan responded with "That is good news, Sergeant Windflower. Who is it?"

"I'm not at liberty to say just yet," said Windflower as his gaze drifted back to the young man. "But when we do make an arrest we will notify your mother. When are you heading back, by the way?"

"My flight's on Wednesday morning from St. John's so I'll probably head into town on Tuesday night. It's been nice having a few days to visit and catch up with people. Especially with Marge, I mean Mrs. Brenton. She was such a good friend of my uncle," said Sheridan.

"Well enjoy the rest of your stay," said Windflower. "And the rest of your day, Mrs. Brenton."

He nodded goodbye to them both and went back to his table. That was strange, thought Windflower. Both of them together and both likely knowing who the murderer was by now. And both of them trying to be as nonchalant as possible. Interesting, thought Windflower.

But he didn't have much time to think for the everyday tornado that was Constable Eddie Tizzard had just burst into the café and was heat-seeking his target, Winston Windflower. When he saw him he rushed over.

"Another cuppa, Sheila please," called out Windflower. "My young Constable here needs to sit and relax for a few minutes."

Chapter Thirty-Seven

Tizzard could barely sit still as Windflower started to outline the events that had just taken place over the last few days. He told Tizzard about Cormier's change of heart and sudden willingness to cooperate, omitting the slight details of cutting off Cormier's pain killers to move things along. He also told him about his meeting with Pomeroy and his team that morning and the plan to arrest Harvey Brenton if Cormier lived up to his promises to talk.

"Wow," said Tizzard, "it's hard to believe that all of this happened in the last twenty-four hours since I saw you."

"Yeah," said Windflower," let's hope that the next twenty-four hours is a little less exciting. If everything goes well with Cormier's interview we should be able to pick Harvey Brenton up some time tomorrow."

"Thanks, Sheila," said Tizzard, as the café owner deposited his cup of coffee on the table between them. He noticed the smile that passed from her to his Boss as she walked away.

Windflower left Tizzard still guessing on that front as he quickly changed the subject. "I hear that the boys picked up a few more teenagers on the weekend. Who was on the town patrol?" he asked.

"Fortier," said Tizzard. "They picked up six of them on Saturday night and brought them home to their parents. One of them was young Maurice Tibbo, the Mayor's nephew," he said.

"Yeah, I heard about that already," said Windflower. "The Mayor's been on the blower to me about it. Maybe this will quiet him down a bit."

"Hope, so," said Tizzard. "We've got enough to do without having to babysit those kids as well. I think they're just bored. Ever since they closed up the rec centre the kids have nowhere to go. So they just hang out at the wharf and look for trouble to get into."

"Anyway, I've got to get back," said Windflower. "Can you come by and see me this afternoon? I've got some paperwork to clear up with you."

"Sure," said Tizzard looking a bit puzzled, "I have to go to Fortune to pick up a package from the skipper on the boat, but I should be back around two."

"Great, I'll see you then," said Windflower as he drained his mug and went up to the counter to pay.

"Oh, coffee's on the house today," said Sheila with a twinkle in her eye. "Got to look after the local constabulary."

"Well, thank you, Ma'am," said Windflower. "It's good to see that we have the respect of the people."

"Well, you have my respect, anyway," said Sheila. "Will I see you later?"

"If you're up for a take-out pizza and a movie at Chez Windflower then you will," replied Windflower.

"I am indeed," said Sheila. "I'll call you after work."

"Ciao," said Windflower as he headed out the door and back to his office.

Monday was always a little hectic at the RCMP detachment, partly because there was a shift change and partly because it was Monday and things were always a bit crazy then.

Windflower waved hello and good bye to three people on the way in or out of the office until he came face to face, or at least his chest to the face of the Mayor of Grand Bank, Francis Tibbo.

"Good morning, Mr. Mayor," said Windflower. "To what do we have the honour of your presence this fine morning?"

"Cut the guff," said Tibbo, "you know why I'm here."

"Come into my office," said Windflower as he waved good morning to an overloaded Betsy bearing files and duty rosters and weekend reports to the photocopier area. She couldn't wave but she smiled her sympathy to Windflower as he closed the door to his office with him and the Mayor inside.

"My brother, and more importantly his wife, are very upset this morning about their son, Maurice, being brought home by the police on Saturday night," Francis Tibbo sputtered.

"Well, that's what we agreed on, wasn't it?" asked Windflower.

"Yes, but maybe we need to go a little softer with this approach," said the Mayor.

"Softer?" asked Windflower. "What do you want us to do? The RCMP are not baby-sitters. What about the parents? Don't they have some responsibility?

"Let's leave the parents out of this for now," retorted Tibbo. "I just know that I don't want any more of them calling my house on Sunday morning to complain about the RCMP."

Windflower realized that this was a dumping session and not a problem solving one so he waited for the Mayor to give him his suggestions as to how to proceed. After listening to his complaints he was not much further ahead but the Mayor seemed a little calmer.

"Okay, I'll talk to my team and see what we can do," said Windflower.

"Thank you, Sergeant," said Tibbo as he made his way out of the office, feeling that once again he had resolved the situation, at least to his satisfaction.

Windflower watched as the Mayor drove off and gave himself the brief luxury of hating the man's guts for about two minutes before he went back to work. He shuffled the paperwork on his desk for a few more minutes before Betsy came in holding a manila file folder.

"Here's the form you wanted, Sergeant," she said, handing him the promotion file. Your portion is Section F. If you want to write something up I can type it in for you."

"Thanks, Betsy, said Windflower."I'll drop it back to you in a few minutes. Also, could you schedule a staff meeting for everyone who's around for two o'clock this afternoon and pick up some donuts or cookies or something?"

"Sure thing, Boss," said Betsy. "Are we celebrating something?"

"I certainly hope so," said Windflower.

Chapter Thirty-Eight

Windflower added his comments in the appropriate section where he extolled Tizzard's virtues and initiative, both crucial elements in the required format to secure approval for the request to move Tizzard from lowly Constable to Corporal. He dropped the file on Betsy's desk and mouthed good bye as she was actively engaged on the phone.

Time to check in on my pal Stoodley, he thought, as he wandered along the back streets to his friend's house.

Howard Stoodley as usual was perched in his sun porch at his easel and he waved Windflower in when he saw him.

"Good morning, Howard, what is that delicious smell?" asked Windflower.

"That my friend is Moira's special moose stew. She left it in the crock pot to warm up just in time for lunch. And seeing that you're here, it must be that time. Come into the kitchen and I'll get us a couple of bowls," said Stoodley.

"I do have impeccable timing," said Windflower, "especially when it comes to food."

Soon both men were heavily engaged in enjoying the fruits of Stoodley's partner's labour.

"This is fabulous!!" exclaimed Windflower. "What kind of spices does she use?"

"It's an old family recipe," said Stoodley. "Moira guards it with her life but I think it's probably an extra dash of good old fashioned

Newfoundland savoury. It just seems to really bring out the flavour of the moose meat."

"Well, give her my compliments," said Windflower as he refused another helping. "I'd die for a cup of tea, though," he said.

"No problem," said Stoodley, "I'll put the kettle on. I wouldn't want a Mountie dying in my kitchen.

"So what's the info that you have?" asked Windflower. "Or maybe I should fill you in first."

"You go first while I make the tea and get us some of that blueberry cake from the fridge for dessert," said Stoodley.

Windflower ran through the events since they last spoke including his run-in with MacIntosh in Marystown. "He was not happy to see me to put it mildly," he said.

"No, and he will be less happy when he gets to St. John's," said Stoodley. "My sources tell me that he is in well over his head and unless he is prepared to blow the whistle on somebody above him he is the one going to wear a lot of the garbage that's been flying around. Even if he doesn't there's going to be a full investigation announced next week by the provincial and federal justice departments. Someone finally got the memo that there's rotten fish in Newfoundland."

"Well that is certainly good news, Howard," said Windflower. "Pomeroy and his crew have suspected for a while that there was direct and indirect interference in their investigations. I found it hard to believe that we didn't even have a working file on Harvey Brenton in our office. That's unheard of and I blame MacIntosh for that."

"Yeah, MacIntosh was certainly part of the problem," said Stoodley, "But my people tell me that he was actually way down on the food chain when it comes to dirty hands."

"How far up does it go?" asked Windflower.

"No one's quite sure, but the investigation is being carried out by the OPP under the direction of the Commissioner's office in the RCMP," said Stoodley.

"They brought the Ontario Provincial Police into this!" exclaimed Windflower. "That means they don't trust anyone in the chain of command."

"Or the province," said Stoodley. "We'll see what happens but one thing's for sure, MacIntosh is not coming back to this area and he'll be lucky if he doesn't end up behind bars himself."

"Well, good riddance to him, I'd say," said Windflower. "Now slide me over a piece of that blueberry cake."

Feeling particularly stuffed, Windflower walked slowly back to his office, arriving there just before two. People were all heading into the meeting room and Windflower went back to his office to drop off his coat. He found a rather nervous looking Tizzard waiting for him.

"Come on, Tizzard. We've got something to celebrate," he said to his visibly relieved colleague. When they got to the meeting room everyone rose to applaud them both.

"I guess good news travels fast, Tizzard," said Windflower.

"I guess so, Boss," said Tizzard.

After giving all the troops an update on the on-going investigation, along with the news that Inspector MacIntosh had been temporarily reassigned which brought smiles and more applause, Windflower brought Tizzard to the front of the room and read his recommendation out loud.

Tizzard blushed but was obviously very proud and thanked his Sergeant for the opportunity to work on such an important and interesting case. After donuts and coffee everyone dispersed to their separate duties and Windflower went back to clean up his desk. At about 3:30 he said goodnight to Betsy and headed home for the day. He deserved a couple of hours off and besides he had to tidy up his house before Sheila came over.

Soon he was humming while vacuuming and dusting and putting away the stacks of books and papers his solitary lifestyle had accumulated. He put clean towels in the bathroom and even put clean sheets on the bed. You never know what might happen, he thought and as an old boy scout, he wanted to be prepared.

Chapter Thirty-Nine

Around 5:30 Sheila called and agreed to meet Windflower at Greco's, the pizza joint at around 6:30 to pick up their half vegetarian, half meat-lovers pizza for their dinner. I guess we really are different, thought Windflower, but we were able to compromise and we both are getting what we want. That has to be a good sign.

Shortly after 6 he called to place their order and after one more quick look around to make sure it was presentable enough he grabbed his coat and headed up to the pizza place. It was a short walk, like most in Grand Bank, but he wanted to get out and get another breath of fresh air so he took the long way around. Past the grand old B+B and down along the wharf where the huge Polish freighter had lain grounded and rusting for the last year. He also saw the RCMP anti-smuggling cutter moored up against the customs shed. All slick, sleek, jet-black and as fast as the wind. It needed to be, he thought, to keep up with the high speed smugglers now patrolling the coast.

Before he knew it he was at the door of Greco's and Sheila was just coming up the street towards him. Together they went inside, grabbed their pizza and started back towards Windflower's bungalow. Soon inside with a slice of their chosen side of the pizza and a glass of cold wine they settled in for Windflower's choice of movie for the evening, "The Dark Knight."

This is nice, thought Windflower as Sheila smuggled against him although the movie was in fact a little too dark for both of them and certainly for the mood that Windflower was in. After another slice of pizza and a refill of their wine, they both agreed to leave Batman and the Joker for another night.

"So you must be pleased with how your investigation is turning out," said Sheila as she followed Windflower into the kitchen with her plate.

"Yes, I'm quite happy so far," said Windflower. "I'm especially pleased about MacIntosh being relieved of his duties, at least for the time being and hopefully for good."

"He is not a very nice man," said Sheila. "I didn't tell you before but he and I had a run-in some time ago. He's the kind of man that just pushes all my wrong buttons. I guess he reminds me a bit of my Dad. You know, a bit bossy and a know-it-all and the attitude that's there's nothing a woman can do that a man can't do better."

"I can see that he had an impression on you," smiled Windflower. "You get red in the face just talking about him."

"Stop teasing, Winston. I know you like to do it but you will never get anywhere with me like that," she said back.

"Now you've got my attention," said Windflower. "Can I offer you a cup of tea or dessert?"

"I'll take my dessert in there," said Sheila, pointing to the bedroom.

"Great idea," said Windflower.

Sheila must have risen and left early thought Windflower when he awoke to his alarm clock at 6:45. The side of the bed where she had laid was still warm and if he reached over he could still smell her essence. He traipsed to the bathroom and saw her goodbye written in lipstick on the mirror. "Good morning Winston. Thank you for everything. Especially dessert!! Sheila."

Windflower smiled as he made his coffee. He smiled as he looked out the window even though the wind and rain made it almost impossible to see across the road. He smiled as he got drenched doing his smudge on his back step. He might just smile all day, he thought.

When he came back inside Windflower noticed that the message light was blinking on his cell phone. He picked it up and dialed into his message box. It was from Pomeroy in Marystown.

"Good morning Windflower, it's Pomeroy. We have talked to Cormier and have his written statement implicating Harvey Brenton in the murder of Elias Martin. We've talked to the Crown Attorney and they're prepared to lay first degree murder charges against him. So you have our okay to pick up Mr. Brenton. Give me a call later to let me know how it goes. Thanks again for your help with this."

Windflower saved the message and sat for a moment just to let all of this sink in. Then he finished up his coffee and grabbed his coat and hat. He was reminded about the wind as soon as he unlatched his front door. It nearly blew off the hinges. Then he got hit in the face with the driving rain like a scattershot of needles biting into his face and eyes. He lowered his head and started off towards work. But despite the weather he still had his smile. Now he had two things worth smiling about.

He splashed into the detachment and after bidding hello to Betsy went back to get himself a coffee and see who was around this morning. Paul Fortier was sitting at the table reading some official looking RCMP publication. "Good morning Paul," said Windflower.

"Morning, Sarge," said Fortier. "You're in a good mood for such an awful looking day."

"I am in a good mood," said Windflower, "because today we get to put one of the true bad guys where he belongs, behind bars. That always makes me feel good."

"I know what you mean," said Fortier. "I wish I could feel as good about rounding up those teenagers and bringing them home to their parents, but the truth is, I don't. I wish we had another way to handle this."

"Yeah, you and me both. And the Mayor too, by the way," said Windflower. "You know I was talking to Tizzard and he had a point. When the rec centre was open we had fewer problems with the teenagers and they weren't just hanging around and drinking. I wonder if there's any way we can get that place up and running again."

"That's a great idea, Boss," said Fortier. "If you talk to the Mayor then maybe me and the new Corporal can see if we can't get some support from the local business community to get it back in operation. We can talk to the Lions and the Kiwanis clubs for starters."

"Tizzard would be good at that," said Windflower.

"Good at what?" asked Tizzard as he came into the room with his mouth stuffed with what looked like the remains of a breakfast sandwich.

"You got a new assignment," said Windflower. "RCMP Liaison Officer on the committee for the new and improved rec centre. Fortier will be your side kick. Let me talk to the Mayor and we'll see if we can't get moving on this. Better than shipping the kids home drunk to their parents."

"That's for sure," said Fortier as he packed up his stuff and left for his vehicle. "I'm on the highway today. Wish me luck," he said. "With this weather I'm probably going to be pulling a moose off somebody's vehicle."

"Good luck," said Windflower and to Tizzard he said "You and I have an appointment with one Harvey Brenton."

"You got the call?" asked Tizzard.

"Yeah, Pomeroy left me a message. Apparently Cormier sang like a canary. We have a statement and a warrant on its way to arrest Mr. Brenton," said Windflower.

"So what are we waiting for?" asked Tizzard.

"I want us to have some back-up in case anything goes wrong. You and I will go together and who else is on today?" Windflower asked.

"Lewis and Lapierre," said Tizzard.

"Okay, round them up and tell them to follow us. Get them to sign out a couple of the heavy guns from the armory. And get body suits for everybody. We don't know what kind of weaponry Harvey Brenton has in that house and I don't want to take any chances. While you organize that I'm going to call the marine patrol and make sure they have someone in the water as well. Brenton's house is right on the water isn't it?" he asked.

"Yes. And he's got a couple of beauty boats as well as a private dock," said Tizzard. "I'll go get Lewis and Lapierre and the suits ready."

"Okay we'll all head out at around 11," said Windflower.

Chapter Forty

The next hour flew by and soon both teams of Mounties were on their way to the Brenton's house. They parked in front and Windflower noticed that there were three cars already in the parking area. Two he recognized, one was Harvey Brenton's and the other belonged to his wife. The third was a red Dodge Caliber, new, with local plates and a rental car sticker on the back bumper.

He told Lewis and Lapierre to get their guns out of the back and to follow close behind him and Tizzard. He and his young partner walked slowly and deliberately to the front door and as they got closer they could hear voices, loud voices. One of them was clearly Harvey Brenton and he was yelling at someone else. Then a loud blast of gunfire and a woman screaming "No", at the top of her lungs. Both Windflower and Tizzard pushed the door open at the same time and crouched down to survey the scene. Lapierre and Lewis came in right behind them with their guns pointing the way.

Standing in the middle of the plush white shag carpet looking ashen and trembling from head to toe was Marge Brenton. She was without her makeup and wearing a short sleeved blouse her bruising and a black eye were obvious. She also started to look much closer to her real age. Lying side by side at her feet were Harvey Brenton bleeding steadily from a gaping chest wound, and a shotgun that must have inflicted that wound.

"Call 911," Windflower shouted to Lapierre as Tizzard called, "Look over here, Sarge."

Windflower ran over to Tizzard who was pointing out through the picture window overlooking the water to a small boat just leaving the dock and heading out to sea towards St. Pierre. "Did you see who it was?" asked Windflower.

"Just a glimpse," said Tizzard. "It looked like a young guy; maybe it was one of Brenton's sons," he replied.

"No, I think it might be Elias Martin's nephew, James Sheridan. Isn't that right, Mrs. Brenton?" Windflower asked. But Marge Brenton remained in her own personal fog, glued to the spot on the carpet where a pool of her husband's blood was starting to collect.

"Lewis, grab some towels out of the bathroom," said Windflower as he bent over Harvey Brenton and started to apply pressure to the gaping wound to try and stem the flow of blood. "And call our boat and get them to pick up our runaway," he shouted at Tizzard.

Soon Lewis was back with a stack of towels that Windflower was quickly using in a desperate attempt to keep him alive until the medics got there. Windflower could faintly hear the sirens in the distance when Harvey Brenton started to convulse and with a great shudder at approximately 11:45 he stopped breathing.

The emergency personnel would try to revive him when they arrived but shortly after their arrival they realized that there was little they could do. "He's dead, Sergeant," said the lead paramedic. "We can't pronounce him but he's not coming back," he said.

"Thanks," said Windflower. "Can you call Doctor Sanjay at the clinic and ask him to come over?" he asked. The lead paramedic nodded agreement and his team started to gather up their equipment. As they were leaving Marge Brenton suddenly woke up from her dream. "It was me," she said.

"What?" asked Windflower who was now feeling like he was in a dream of his own.

"It was me," Marge Brenton said again, this time louder and firmer. "I killed him."

Windflower just stared at Marge Brenton until Tizzard roused him with "Boss, the marine unit's got our guy. What should they do with him?"

"Get them to bring him and the boat back here," said Windflower. "Sometimes people are more eager to tell the truth at the scene of a crime," he said.

Windflower barked out orders to his team. "Lewis, you take Mrs. Brenton into the kitchen and keep her company. Tizzard, you are in charge of securing the crime scene. Call Fortier and tell him to bring over the camera, and the tape, and the fingerprint kit to start with. Lapierre, I want you to take a statement from the marine crew when they get here and then hold young Mr. Sheridan in the dining room. I am going to get cleaned up."

Windflower needed to get rid of Harvey Brenton's blood but he also needed a few minutes to clear his head. He didn't want to make any mistakes in dealing with this new and disturbing turn of events. "Okay, he said to himself, "We have two suspects and a confession. Let's talk to the one who hasn't confessed first."

Chapter Forty-One

Within fifteen minutes the RCMP jetty was docked alongside the late Harvey Brenton's wharf and Lapierre was getting the statement from the marine patrol about their brief but exciting chase and capture. Soon James Sheridan was being escorted up the stairs to the house and into the dining room.

"Good afternoon, James," said Windflower as Sheridan came into the room. Take a seat." Lapierre stood to the side and took out his notebook. Windflower nodded his agreement to Lapierre and looked directly into James Sheridan's eyes.

"So what happened here, James? And why were you running?" he asked.

"So is he dead?" asked Sheridan.

"Yes," said Windflower, seeing no reason to hold anything back.

"I did it," said Sheridan. "I killed Harvey Brenton."

For the second time that day Windflower was gob-smacked. He stared for more than a few moments at James Sheridan.

"Boss," said Tizzard from behind him, waking Windflower up for the second time that day. "Boss," said Tizzard a little more loudly, "Doctor Sanjay is here."

"Stay here," said Windflower to Lapierre, "and make sure that Mr. Sheridan stays here too."Tizzard, I want you to take Mr. Sheridan's photo and get his fingerprints."

To Sheridan he said "We will have more questions for you later," and went back out to the living room where Doctor Sanjay was bent over Harvey Brenton's lifeless body.

"Well?" asked Windflower.

"Well, he certainly is dead," said the doctor. "I'll have a closer look when I get back to the clinic but I think it's safe to say that Harvey Brenton died of complications as a result of a gunshot wound. He lost a lot of blood by the looks of it but that's not what killed him. I suspect that given the location of the bullet hole that it probably went through his lung and nicked his aorta. Sooner rather than later that cuts off the flow of blood to the heart and the patient succumbs. You can survive a lot of things with a gunshot wound, but that's not one of them," he concluded.

Looking back at Windflower he asked "Who did it?"

"Not sure yet," said Windflower, "but I've got two people trying to confess."

"An interesting dilemma," said the doctor. "As long as you're sure that one of them did it, then you're okay."

"Yeah, I guess so," said Windflower. "I just have to figure out who's lying."

"Well, good luck with that," said Doctor Sanjay. "My ambulance crew is outside waiting to take the body back if you're done here," he said.

"Are you finished Fortier?" Windflower asked.

"I think we're done with the body," said Fortier. "We've got tons of pictures. We'll need a little more time to gather up and id all the evidence, but otherwise we're good."

"Have you dusted the weapon for prints?" asked Windflower. "Can you also see if there is any powder residue or traces on the hands and clothing of our two witnesses?"

"Ok, Boss," said Fortier.

"Thanks, Doc, for getting here so fast," said Windflower. "You can take the body now. Make sure your guys are careful with the scene."

"No problem, Sergeant," said the doctor.

Tizzard came out of the dining room and walked up to Windflower. "So what's next?" he asked.

"Finish the job here with Fortier and help him secure the scene. Once you're done that you can come back with me to the detachment. Fortier, I want you to stay on-site until I can send someone back to relieve you."

"Okay," said Tizzard and Fortier nodded and continued his work bagging up some of the towels that Windflower had used to sop up Harvey Brenton's blood.

Windflower went back into the kitchen where Marge Brenton was sitting stoically under the watchful eye of Constable Lewis. The colour in her face had returned but instead of making her look better it only served to highlight her shiner and bruises. They looked worse than ever.

"Mrs. Brenton," said Windflower, "You are now a suspect in the death of your husband. I am going to get Constable Tizzard to take your picture and your fingerprints here and then we are going to take you back to the Grand Bank detachment office for questioning." Marge Brenton did not respond so Windflower went back to see James Sheridan in the dining room.

"Mr. Sheridan," he said. "You are now a suspect in the death of Harvey Brenton. We are going to take your picture and your fingerprints here and then we are going to take you back to the Grand Bank detachment office for questioning." James Sheridan had no response either.

Windflower motioned Lapierre outside and said "I'll send Tizzard right over when he's done with Mrs. Brenton. Once Tizzard is finished you can take Sheridan back to the detachment. Put him in the cell in the very back. Ok?" Windflower asked.

"Ok, Sarge," said Lapierre.

Windflower passed Tizzard as he was just leaving the kitchen and directed him to the dining room for his next task. Then he walked calmly into the kitchen and sat across the kitchen table from Marge Brenton. "So, Mrs. Brenton, said Windflower, "Tell me what happened here."

Marge Brenton crossed her hands in her lap and in a low but solid-sounding voice began with," It's never been easy living with Harvey. His temper has always been out of control and while it has seldom been this bad, when he lost it I usually got the worst of it."

"This," she said, pointing to the bruises on her arms and touching her tender eye socket, "was because I talked to you about Elias Martin. Harvey didn't like anyone to know his business. Whenever I crossed that line of his, this is what happened."

"I have stayed quiet about it for a long time because I was thinking about the children. But they knew all about it. My son wanted me to leave and come live with his family, but I couldn't do it. This was and is my life."

"This time," she said, "It was James who was encouraging me to leave. He wanted me to come to Ontario for a while with him and his mother, Georgette. He didn't want Harvey to be able to hurt me anymore. I told him I couldn't do that either. James had also figured out that Harvey was responsible for his uncle's death and wanted to confront him about it. I thought I had him talked out of that and he had just come by this morning to say goodbye before he went back home."

"Unfortunately for all of us Harvey decided to drop home this morning to pick up something he had left behind. When he saw James and me he went crazy. And of course James was just as bad, yelling at Harvey and calling him a murderer and a wife beater. Harvey went bananas and I thought he really was going to kill James. So I went down to the basement and got Harvey's shotgun. I was hoping that I could threaten Harvey long enough so that James could escape. So I pointed the gun at him, I didn't even know it was loaded and when he came towards me I accidently pulled the trigger and the gun went off."

"Harvey just dropped to the floor and I screamed. When I heard somebody outside, I yelled at James to get out and take the speedboat back into Grand Bank and then go home as quickly as he could. He didn't want to but he took off when you busted the door open." At this last statement Marge Brenton kind of just crumpled and her head fell weeping into her hands.

"Thank you, Mrs. Brenton," said Windflower. "That will be enough for now. We'll have more questions later. Constable Lewis will take you back to the detachment shortly."

Motioning Lewis outside he said "Wait a few minutes and then take Mrs. Brenton back to the office. Put her in the very front cell, Ok?"

"Ok, Boss," said Lewis.

Chapter Forty-Two

Soon only Windflower, Tizzard and Fortier were left at the Brenton house. Harvey Brenton's remains were now being off-loaded at the back door of the Grand Bank Medical Clinic and both Marge Brenton and James Sheridan were safely secured in their holding cells back at the RCMP Detachment.

"We're taking your car, Fortier," said Windflower. "Tizzard and I are heading back and I'll send someone back to relieve you later. Until we find out exactly what happened here I want this scene absolutely secure."

"No problem," said Fortier. "I'd rather be nice and warm in here than out on the highway today, anyway."

"Shoot," said Windflower. "I forgot about that. I'll have to call Marystown to get some backup. You drive, Tizzard, but take your time. We've had enough deaths for a while around here."

Tizzard has his first brief smile for a while and simply nodded to his superior as he pulled the cruiser out from the front of the Brenton household. Windflower pulled out his cell phone and called Betsy at the office.

"Good morning, Sergeant," said Betsy.

"Betsy, can you find out who is replacing Inspector MacIntosh in Marystown and ask him to call me right away?" asked Windflower. "Tizzard and I are on our way back. Have Lewis and Lapierre delivered our guests?"

"Yes sir," said Betsy. "They're in their cells and the boys are watching over them carefully."

"Thanks, Betsy," said Windflower as he hung up.

Just before arriving at the detachment Windflower's phone rang. "Windflower," he answered.

'Windflower, it's Kevin Arsenault. I'm taking over from Macintosh as Acting Inspector. I hear you've had some excitement over there," he said.

"Yes, Inspector you could call it that," said Windflower as he gave the Acting Inspector a rundown of the day's events so far. "I guess we're going to need some back up for a day or two until we get sorted out," he said.

"I thought you might," said Arsenault. "I've got two cars on the way over from Marystown, one for highway and one for your local patrol. Will that be enough?" he asked.

"That's fine for now. Thank you, sir," said Windflower.

"I'm on my way over there now as well," said Arsenault. "I have a background in C.I.D. and as a major crime investigator. Maybe I could assist with the interviews?" he asked.

"That would be great," said Windflower. "We can use all the help we can get." Windflower thought that this was certainly a pleasant change from the gruff dictatorial style of Inspector MacIntosh, someone wanting to help rather to take over or take credit. "I look forward to meeting you," he said.

'I'll see you in about an hour," said Inspector Arsenault as he hung up.

Windflower went into the foyer of the detachment and said good morning to Betsy who was on the phone and pointing to the blinking panel of her switchboard. As soon as she could Betsy put down her headset and simply said to Windflower, "There's coffee in the back."

"Thanks Betsy," said Windflower as he and Tizzard made their way back to the small lunchroom pausing only to nod at Lewis and Lapierre standing guard and to peek at their guests who were both in quiet reflection. With a sigh of relief Windflower poured himself and Tizzard a cup of coffee and they both sat for a few moments in silence. Each of them processing the non-stop adventure they had both just been through.

Finally Windflower broke the silence by saying "A bit more excitement than we had planned, eh Tizzard?"

"Yeah, I'd say," said Tizzard. "Who do you think did it Boss?" he asked, posing the question that had been on his mind for the last hour.

"Well, it was certainly one of them," said Windflower, "and they both had valid reasons for wanting Harvey Brenton dead. But at this point I really don't know. It looks like they both may have been involved but until we get some more info it's hard to know who pulled the trigger."

"That reminds me, I better get busy processing those fingerprints from the gun and storing some of the evidence. I'll get right on it," said Tizzard.

When Tizzard had left Windflower dialed the number of the café and was soon on the line with Sheila.

"Is everything okay? More importantly are you okay?" asked Sheila. "The word on the street or at least in the café is that Harvey Brenton is dead.

"First of all I'm fine. It's been quite a morning," Windflower answered. "And yes without divulging too many state secrets I can say that Mr. Brenton is indeed dead. But please don't ask me any more questions right now, I don't have many answers."

"I understand," said Sheila."I'm just glad you're okay."

"I am fine, better now," said Windflower, "For some reason I feel better when I talk to you. I had a wonderful evening last night. Thank you."

"Thank you, Winston," said Sheila. "I had a great time too. Sorry I had to leave so early but I had to open up this morning."

"There'll be lots of mornings to sleep in," said Windflower.

"I hope so," laughed Sheila. "I know you'll be busy with this stuff for a while but give me a call when you can."

"I will Sheila, goodbye," said Windflower. Windflower went out to help Tizzard with his evidence bags and watched him set up the fingerprint testing equipment. Before he could see the results Betsy poked her head in and said "Inspector Arsenault is here, Sergeant."

"Thanks Betsy," said Windflower. "I'm on my way. And on his way out he shouted to Tizzard, "I want any results, anything you find, as soon as you find it!!"

Windflower walked into his office and his new superior officer rose to greet him. Acting Inspector Kevin Arsenault was almost as tall as Windflower with short cropped salt and pepper hair and a handshake that showed both strength and confidence. He was in his late 40's, maybe a well-preserved early 50's with a slim but solid build and a smile that made Windflower feel instantly comfortable.

After brief pleasantries, Inspector Arsenault asked, "Have you interviewed the witnesses yet?"

"Just Marge Brenton briefly and James Sheridan long enough for him to confess," said Windflower. He gave a short synopsis to Arsenault and added that, "it didn't feel right doing full interviews at the crime scene. I thought it would be better and more professional to do it on our own turf."

"Good idea," said Arsenault. "Can I see them now?"

"Sure," said Windflower and he rose and led the Inspector down the corridor where the cells were located.

Going to the back he said "Here's James Sheridan," pointing to a now dejected looking young man sitting on the bed in his small cell. Moving to the front area he pointed out Marge Brenton who was standing at the back of her cell, thinking or maybe even praying.

"Thank you," was all Inspector Arsenault said after seeing the prisoners. "Can we go back to your office?"

When they got there Arsenault said "I think we should move them to Marystown for interrogation. We'll need better security than you have here and I don't think you have a female officer to supervise Mrs. Brenton, do you?" he asked.

"No, sir," said Windflower. "But can I come with you? I have a lot of the background information and I think it would be good to have continuity on this case. If that's okay with you."

"No problem, Sergeant," said Arsenault. "I know that some people had problems in the past but I just want you know one thing. I am interested in justice and in seeing justice done. I don't care who gets credit and there's always enough blame to go around. I want you involved in this case because you can help secure justice. So yes, you can come and you can work under me for the interrogations. Do you have anyone you can leave in charge here?"

"I have a guy, Tizzard, who I'm recommending for Corporal," said Windflower. "He can handle it."

"Great," said Arsenault. "A few questions before we continue. Did either of our suspects ask for lawyers yet?"

"Not yet," said Windflower. "But I haven't told them they're being charged with anything yet, either."

"One step at a time, Windflower. Until they ask, which at some point they will, it's easier getting answers than when there's a solicitor in the room. Trust me on that," said Arsenault. "It also looks like Marge Brenton has been beaten up pretty bad. Has she been given a medical examination?" he asked.

"No," said Windflower, "but we can take her to the clinic here in town before we go to Marystown. Her family doctor works there. He's also our chief medical officer of health and coroner."

"Ok," said Arsenault. "And the young guy, Sheridan, what kind of background have you got on him? Does he have a criminal record?" he asked.

"I don't know but we can certainly do a check right now. And I know his mother well enough to talk to her about her son. Let me go and get my secretary on the records check right now," said Windflower as he went to relay the request to Betsy.

"Betsy, can you do a CR check on James Sheridan and also call Dr. Sanjay at the clinic to see if he can do an exam on Marge Brenton right away? Thanks, Betsy," said Windflower.

"Okay," said Windflower to his new Inspector as he came back into his office, "we're moving on the criminal records check and getting an appointment for Mrs. Brenton at the clinic."

"Great," said Inspector Arsenault. "I'll head back over to Marystown to get everything set up and you come over with our guests when you're ready."

After Inspector Arsenault had left Windflower felt an overwhelming urge to just lie down and go to sleep. Instead he went to the back and poured himself another coffee. This was going to be a long day and he had indeed many miles to go before he could go to sleep.

Chapter Forty-Three

When he came back to his office Betsy was waiting for him. "Doctor Sanjay is waiting for Mrs. Brenton whenever you want to send her over. He said to bring her around back to the ambulance doors," said Betsy. "And I've got a printout on James Sheridan."

"Thanks Betsy," said Windflower as he sat at his desk to go through the report. "Can you ask Tizzard to come in and see me when he's got a chance?"

Windflower saw the top caption on the print out: James Elias Sheridan, named after his uncle. Date of birth: Jan 14, 1984. Windflower's quick math made that 27. Charged with manslaughter in Brampton in May, 2005. Found not criminally responsible because of mental illness. Remanded for treatment to the secure ward of the Brockville Psychiatric Institution. Released in February, 2009 to the care of Georgette Sheridan with conditions that he maintain medication levels and check in twice a year with a court appointed psychiatrist.

"Wow," said Windflower out loud.

"Something exciting?" asked Tizzard as he came into Windflower's office.

Windflower just handed the record over to Tizzard who whistled through his teeth as he looked it over.

"Wow is right," said Tizzard.

"Tizzard, I want you to do some in-depth research on this one. Get the whole story. Talk to the guys who ran the case in

Ontario, probably OPP but they might be local cops. And we'll want this right away."

Tizzard stood up to leave but Windflower motioned for him to sit down. "That's not why I called you in," he said. "I am going to Marystown to help Inspector Arsenault with the case there. In my absence I want you to be in charge. We've got two cars coming from Marystown to help out and the duty rosters are all set up. If you have any questions about the office then talk to Betsy. She knows everything. If there are any problems, anything at all, I want to know about it. I'll send a memo around to everybody about it."

Tizzard just sat there looking at Windflower dumbfounded. "Well don't just sit there. Get to work," said Windflower. "The first thing you can do is arrange for Mrs. Brenton to get up to see Dr. Sanjay at the clinic. Betsy set it up so talk to her."

"Yes, sure thing, Boss," said Tizzard as still in a bit of a daze he went out to see Betsy.

"And send Betsy back in to see me," yelled Windflower at Tizzard's disappearing back.

When Betsy returned he handed her the report. "Can you e-mail this to Inspector Arsenault and call him to give him the details. You can tell him we're doing some more checking on our end. Also Betsy would you prepare a memo for my signature assigning Constable Tizzard as my acting replacement. I have to go to Marystown to help out there and he will be in charge in my absence."

"Yes, Sergeant," said Betsy. "I'll get right on it."

"And Betsy, I know I can count on you to help Tizzard out and if there are any problems you can't handle feel free to give me a call," said Windflower.

"Thank you, sir," said Betsy beaming now at the confidence that her boss had placed in her. "You can count on me."

Windflower busied himself with paperwork until Tizzard came in to inform him that Dr. Sanjay had completed the examination and Mrs. Brenton was back in her holding cell. "She's wearing a sling on her right arm," said Tizzard, "and Dr. Sanjay wants you to call him."

"Thanks, Tizzard," said Windflower. "Could you assign someone to drive one car and I'll take another to transport the prisoners?"

As Tizzard nodded and left Windflower picked up the phone and called Dr. Sanjay at the clinic.

"Winston," said the doctor. "I wish we could find time to see each other under more favourable circumstances. I miss our Scotch and chess evenings."

"Me too," said Windflower. "Soon, Vijay, I promise. What have you got for me?"

"Mrs. Brenton was quite badly beaten this time, there are bruises all over her body. She must have quite a high tolerance for pain," said the doctor.

"Anything particular to note?" asked Windflower. "Tizzard says she has her arm in a sling."

"Her right arm is badly sprained in a couple of places. It may be even be broken but I didn't have time to do x-rays. Your man

Tizzard was insistent that the process be completed quickly," said Dr. Sanjay.

"We can look after that in Marystown," said Windflower. "Listen, Doc, she's your patient. Do you think she could have killed her husband?"

"I guess anything is possible and she certainly had good reason to want him gone, but I would have my doubts. First of all this is not the first or second or even third time this has happened. Battered women can occasionally rise up but in my professional experience they too seldom do. Some misguided sense of loyalty, even love keeps them tied to their man, no matter how badly they treat them," said the doctor.

"That is sad," said Windflower. "Anyway, Doc, thanks for your help as usual. And I hope that chess and your finest scotch await us soon."

"That is a pleasant thought on such an unpleasant day," said Doctor Sanjay as he rang off.

"Your cars await you, Sarge," said Tizzard as he poked his head into Windflower's office.

"Thanks, Tizzard," said Windflower. "I just have to run home and throw a few things in a bag and I'll be right back."

Windflower raced home and stuffed his overnight bag with a change of clothes, shaving gear and a few toiletries. He threw the bag in the trunk of his car and went back to pick up his passenger for the trip to Marystown. When he got there Lapierre was just escorting James Sheridan into his car.

"I'll see you over there," said Windflower.

He went inside and found Tizzard leading Mrs. Brenton out of her cell. "I'll take over from here," said Windflower and he offered his arm to Marge Brenton who took it and followed alongside him to his car. When she was safely inside the back seat he went back to say goodbye to Betsy and talk to Tizzard.

"Okay, Tizzard, you're in charge now. Will you call Marystown and tell them we are on the way?" he asked.

"No problem, Boss," said Tizzard looking pretty pleased about the situation. "Good luck in Marystown."

"Thanks, Tizzard," said Windflower as he pulled out of the parking lot and noticed that the rain had finally slowed down enough for a rainbow to appear in the distant sky. Maybe a good omen, thought Windflower. I sure hope so.

Chapter Forty-Four

The ride to Marystown was uneventful and Windflower was surprised when he remembered that he hadn't seen a moose for quite some time. That was unusual. But he knew they were out there and if you let your guard down that's exactly the time they would reappear. So Windflower remained vigilant and soon was back at the Marystown detachment. Funny, he thought, I didn't think I'd be back here so soon.

He waited in the parking lot as Lapierre took James Sheridan in through the lock-up door and then left Marge Brenton in the car when he went inside to check on procedures. Sheridan was already being led down the corridor when Windflower opened the door and was greeted by the Corporal in charge.

"You must be Sergeant Windflower. I'm Stan Hopewell. We've sent Sheridan on to booking and if you want to bring the lady in we can look after her in here," said the Corporal pointing to a small waiting area just off the front desk."

"Thanks," said Windflower as he went back out to get Marge Brenton and with her once again gripping his arm he led her into the lock up area.

Once inside Hopewell offered to take over. "We can take it from here," he said. "Constable Vernon," pointing to a petite RCMP officer sitting at the desk in the waiting area, "and I will look after Mrs. Brenton. Inspector Arsenault is expecting you in Boardroom D on the second floor. Just take the elevator on the other side of this section and turn right when you get off."

"Thanks," said Windflower as he left the lock up area through the door in back and went up the elevator. When he arrived at Boardroom D Inspector Arsenault was waiting for him.

"Windflower," said Arsenault. "Take a seat and take a weight off the world. Have you eaten anything today?"

Windflower had to think but then realized that he couldn't remember. "I don't think so, sir," he said. "I guess you really can live on caffeine and adrenaline."

"Not for long," said Arsenault. "I want you to decompress Sergeant. I'll get my assistant Louise to book you a room at the hotel and I want you to go and relax for a few hours. We've got the prisoners locked up and they will probably want some sleep as well. Have a cold drink, grab something to eat, have a shower. If you can sleep that would be even better. Nothing's going to happen tonight so you won't miss anything. I'll see you here at 8 o'clock and we'll get to work. Ok?"

Feeling absolutely drained, Windflower nodded yes. Arsenault introduced him to Louise who booked him a room at the Marystown Motel and arranged for someone to drive him over. Windflower checked in to the hotel and went to the restaurant for a bite to eat. He ordered a burger and fries and a milkshake and devoured it when it arrived. He went back to his room and spent ten minutes soaking up the hot spray in the shower. Afterwards he thought he would just lie on the bed for a minute.

When Windflower woke up his blinking bedside clock said 7:00. He couldn't figure out if it was pm or am so he opened the curtains in his room and was greeted by what else, fog? But at least he could tell it was morning because it was light. Wow, he thought, I guess I really needed the sleep.

After a quick shower and shave he walked back over to the detachment. It wasn't far and Windflower needed both the exercise and the time to clear his foggy brain. He decided to call Sheila along the way.

"Good morning, Mug-Up," said Sheila's cheery voice.

"Good morning, Sheila," said Windflower. "How are you this morning?"

"I'm just fine, Winston. Where are you? I tried to call you last night at home and on your cell phone."

"Oh, sorry, Sheila," said Windflower. "I'm in Marystown. I am going to help out with the investigation from here for a few days. Sorry I didn't call last night. When I got to the hotel I just collapsed. Didn't wake up until a little while ago."

"Well I'm glad you're safe and it sounds like you needed a good night's sleep. How long will you be in Marystown?" Sheila asked.

"Don't know for sure," said Windflower. "A few days at least, I suspect."

"I'm glad you called, Winston. Most of all to know you're all right but also to tell you about something. I don't know if it means anything but Marie in the café, you know Marie?" she asked.

"The older lady, a little slow?" asked Windflower.

"That's her," said Sheila. "But Marie's not as slow as people think. She may not talk a lot but she's learned to be a good listener. Anyway after the word got around about Harvey Brenton's death Marie said to me, 'I wonder if they had anything to do with it'. When I asked her who she meant, she said Marge

Brenton and that young man that was with her at the café the other day."

"What else did she say?" asked Windflower.

"Marie said they were talking about how they might get rid of something. The man said it was best to do it at sea. Marie said she didn't hear much more because they would clam up whenever she came close," said Sheila.

"That is very interesting," said Windflower. "Do you think you could drive Marie over here after work today? I'm sure the Inspector would like to ask her a few more questions. And I'm prepared to buy you and her dinner if you can do it."

"Well I'm sure Marie will be delighted to come and I am too to get dinner with my favourite Mountie," said Sheila.

"Great. I'll expect you around 5 today then," said Windflower. "I'm really glad I got a chance to talk with you, Sheila. I miss you."

"I miss you too," said Sheila.

Windflower had a little extra jump in his step for the last part of his walk. He had good news to pass along to his new Boss and he had a visit with Sheila to look forward to at the end of his day. Not too bad, he thought.

Chapter Forty-Five

Luckily for Windflower and for the entire Marystown RCMP the Tim Horton's coffee shop was right on the path between the hotel and the detachment. Windflower stopped in and had a toasted "everything" bagel with cream cheese and a large coffee. As he sat and enjoyed his breakfast he mentally prepared himself for the day by recounting the last week quickly in his mind. A lot has happened, and still more to come he thought. Finishing his coffee and placing his garbage in the receptacle he completed the last short leg of his trip to work and was soon sitting outside of Inspector Arsenault's office waiting for his superior to finish up another meeting.

When Windflower went in to the office he was introduced to the Inspector's second in command, Staff Sergeant William Ford. "Call me Bill," said the Staff Sergeant to Windflower as they shook hands.

Windflower was happy to pass along his news about Marie that he had heard from Sheila that morning.

"Good," said Arsenault. "Bill has been down to check on our guests this morning. How are they doing?"

"They seem to have gotten a bit of sleep and now that Mr. Sheridan has his medication he is calmed down quite a bit, " said Ford.

Arsenault nodded to his 2 IC and said to Windflower, "Since you are the expert on this file, Windflower, why don't you walk us through your involvement. Take it from the beginning and try and give us as much as you can. Remember we're coming in cold, although we are quite familiar with one character, Patrick Cormier, aren't we Ford?"

"We certainly are," said Ford. "We'd all be quite happy around here never to see him again."

"Cormier is a character all right," said Windflower. "But finding him was a key to cracking the case against Harvey Brenton." Windflower then went on for most of the next two hours telling his new colleagues about his recent history with this case and answering their questions. When he had finished Inspector Arsenault suggested a short break and Ford took Windflower to the small cafeteria in the basement of the building for a coffee.

"So you've had a pretty exciting couple of weeks," said Ford as they got their coffee and took a seat at a table in the corner of the cafeteria.

"Yes," said Windflower. "Things are usually so slow in Grand Bank that you wish that they would heat up every so often, but this latest period has been remarkable. Makes you long for a few days of peace and quiet."

"Yeah, I bet," said Ford. "Working with Arsenault is always a bit of an adventure though. He likes to stay busy."

"How long have you been with him?" asked Windflower?

"I guess it must be seven years now," said Ford. "I worked with him in Montreal when he was with major crimes and we both got transferred here to work C.I.D. three years ago. He's a good guy to work for, a real straight arrow," he continued. "You always know where you stand with Arsenault, and it had better be on his right side."

"Good to know," said Windflower. "It wasn't easy with his predecessor."

"MacIntosh?" asked Ford. "He was a snake. You won't find too many people sorry to see the last of him either. Cormier and MacIntosh in one week, you've made a lot of instant friends around here," laughed Ford.

Windflower laughed too as they finished their coffees and went back to Inspector Arsenault's office. He was still on the phone so Windflower used the time to check in with Betsy in Grand Bank.

"Good morning, Betsy," said Windflower. "How are things going in Grand Bank?"

"Hi Sergeant," said Betsy. "This place is a nuthouse today. We keep getting calls from the media who want to know what's going on and Tizzard is bouncing around like a kangaroo trying to be helpful. I wish he would just get out of my way," she said.

"Is he around there now?" asked Windflower.

"No, thank goodness, I mean sorry, no," said Betsy. "He's gone to the Mug-Up but he'll be back soon. Can I get him to call you?"

"That would be great, Betsy," said Windflower."And you can refer any media calls to Marystown. Just tell them that it's being handled out of here. Once they know that they'll stop bugging you. Well, that's it for me. I'll check in again later today."

"Okay, sir," said Betsy. "I'll give Tizzard the message to call you when he gets back."

Louise said to Windflower and Ford, "He's ready for you again," and opened the door to Inspector Arsenault's office.

"Welcome back, gentlemen," said Arsenault. "Let's talk about our two suspects. First of all, Mrs. Marge Brenton. Married to a now dead violent man and a victim of domestic abuse. How long's that been going on, Windflower?" he asked.

"As long as anyone can remember," said Windflower. "Doctor Sanjay said that there were at least two other major instances that he's aware of and it's probably been going on to some degree since they were married," said Windflower. "Sanjay says that the latest bout was the worst he'd seen and that she had much more damage than appeared on the surface. She has at least a sprained arm that we need to have checked out. The doctor thinks it might be broken," he said.

"Interesting," said Ford. "It might be difficult for a woman with a sprained or broken arm to hold or point a shotgun."

"That is interesting," said Arsenault. "So we know that Mrs. Brenton was not happy about being beaten up again, that she felt badly about Elias Martin's death and her husband's role in it, and she had a discussion with her co-suspect James Sheridan that might have had something to do with how Harvey Brenton ended up dead. That's a good start. What about James Sheridan, Windflower?" he asked.

"Well sir, we know about his criminal record and his medical diagnosis. But we don't know much about what really happened with the manslaughter case or what he's been doing for the last three years. I've got Tizzard checking up on his case with the people in Ontario and I need to call his mother, Georgette Sheridan, at some point. I thought it might be better to interview Sheridan first, Inspector. That might help me know what areas to probe his mother on. Also I'm pretty sure that as soon as I talk to his mother, we'll have a lawyer with us," said Windflower.

"Good thinking, Windflower," said Arsenault. "But I think we'll get one shot at each of them without a lawyer. Once we start picking at them they'll want legal advice. That's not really a problem as long as we can keep them separate."

"Where are we on forensics?" asked Ford.

"I've got a call into Tizzard. I expect to have a report on fingerprints on the weapon and our suspects by the end of the day," said Windflower.

"Great," said Arsenault. "I'll get Louise to get our suspects moved into separate interview rooms and we'll get back together at around 1:30. Fordy, I want you to take notes and Windflower since you know them both I want you to be the lead so think about how you want to approach them. We'll start with the kid. Ok?" he asked as a way to dismiss his troops for lunch.

Both Windflower and Ford nodded and left the office.

"Do you want to walk over to the mall?" asked Ford. "There's a Chinese takeout that's not too bad."

"Great," said Windflower, but his mind was certainly not on food. He was already thinking about how he was going to interview his two suspects.

Chapter Forty-Six

Ford and Windflower ambled over to the mini-mall where the Chinese takeout was located and were soon sitting on a bench with their laps full of greasy fried rice, some vegetable combination that was heavy on carrots and a large oblong egg roll perched on top. Both had wisely declined the offer of soggy chicken balls with a red goopy sauce that looked like it had the texture of heavy grade motor oil.

But to Windflower's surprise it actually tasted pretty good and he told his colleague so. "Yeah, I know," said Ford. "It looks like crap and I suspect it's not very good for you, but it tastes great. Enjoy."

"Wanna grab a coffee at Timmy's?" asked Ford when they had finished their lunch.

"Sure," said Windflower. "That would be great."

At the Tim Horton's a steady parade of RCMP officers nodded or winked to Ford and Windflower. This was clearly as close as you could get in Marystown to the Mountie's hangout. Windflower and Ford sat in the window and watched the cavalcade of motor vehicles go through the drive through.

"Every Mountie's dream," said Ford.

"What?" asked Windflower.

"To retire and open a Tim Horton's," laughed Ford. "I guess we should get back."

When they got back Louise told them that Marge Brenton was in Interview Room # 4 and James Sheridan was in Room # 2. She said Arsenault was still on the phone but would be with them soon. After a few minutes Arsenault walked out of his office and said "Ok, boys, let's go do our interviews. We'll do Marge Brenton first. You ready, Windflower?"

"Yes, sir," said Windflower as they took the stairs to the basement and walked up to Interview Room # 4. They peered through the one-way glass window at Marge Brenton who was sitting nervously at the table. One by one they entered the room and Arsenault nodded to Windflower to begin.

"Good afternoon Mrs. Brenton. You remember me, I'm Sergeant Winston Windflower. These are my colleagues Inspector Kevin Arsenault and Staff Sergeant William Ford. We want to ask you some further questions about the death of your husband, Mrs. Brenton. Are you comfortable; would you like some water or a cup of tea?"

"No thank you, Sergeant," said Marge Brenton. "I already told you what happened. I killed Harvey. I shot him. I don't know what else you want to know. And what happened to James? Is he gone home yet? Nobody will tell me anything."

"Well, you did tell me a little about what happened," said Windflower, ignoring the references to James Sheridan, "but my colleagues haven't heard your story yet and they may have some questions for you."

"What about James? Why won't anybody tell me anything about him? I hope that you still haven't got him locked up somewhere. He didn't do anything. I already told you that I did it," said Marge Brenton, sounding a bit more agitated.

"If you tell us what we want to know, I'll tell you about James," said Windflower, looking to Arsenault who gave his nod as approval. "So why don't you start by telling my friends here what you told me yesterday morning at your house."

"Well," said Marge Brenton. "It's pretty simple. There was an argument between Harvey and James and I got worried so I got Harvey's gun. I tried to get Harvey to back off but he wouldn't and the gun went off," she said.

"What time did James arrive that morning?" asked Windflower.

"I guess it was about quarter to 10,"said Marge Brenton.

"And what did you and he talk about?" Windflower asked.

"James still wanted me to leave and go back with him," Marge Brenton answered.

"Did you talk about his uncle, Elias Martin?" asked Windflower.

"Yes," said Marge Brenton. "James was close to his uncle and blamed Harvey for his death. I tried to get him to let it go but he was still pretty angry."

"Do you know how to use a gun?" asked Arsenault.

Marge Brenton turned to face him and said sternly, "I could fire a shotgun when I was eight years old. By twelve I could bring home a brace of turrs for supper any day of the week."

"How's your arm?" asked Arsenault.

"It's a little stiff, but it's fine," said Marge Brenton.

"We're going to send you over to the hospital for x-rays when we're done here. Doctor Sanjay wants to make sure that it isn't broken," said Windflower.

Marge Brenton made no response to this comment but without thinking about it rubbed her arm beneath its sling.

"I have another question, Mrs. Brenton," said Arsenault. "Harvey Brenton has been likely doing this," and he pointed to her arm, "for years."

"Why did you decide all of a sudden to kill him? Why not any of the other times?"

Marge Brenton looked at the Inspector wearily "I said I shot him, Inspector. I didn't say I meant to kill him. It was an accident," she said coldly.

Turning back to Windflower she said, "I've answered your questions, now where's James? What's going on?"

Windflower quickly glanced a peek at Arsenault who was making no move to slow him down so he said, "James Sheridan is in custody. He claims to have shot Harvey Brenton as well, Mrs. Brenton."

All three men in the room watched closely for Marge Brenton's reaction to this news. But without even pretending to be surprised she said "That's ridiculous. I have already told you what happened. I killed Harvey. That boy is just lying to try and protect me. You have to let him go," she said.

"I'm afraid we can't do that," said Windflower. "Were you aware that James Sheridan has committed a violent act in the past?"

"That was years ago and you can't use that because he was sick." Marge Brenton was growing visibly upset. "I think it would be better if I had a lawyer. I want to get out of here."

"Very well, Mrs. Brenton we'll make arrangements for that," said Windflower. "But we have a few more questions first."

"Not without my lawyer," said Marge Brenton and she clasped her hands in front of her on the table as if to signify that the interview, at least from her perspective, was over.

"Staff Sergeant Ford, will you ensure that Mrs. Brenton gets back to her holding cell and is provided access to her legal counsel," said Arsenault.

"Yes, sir," said Ford as he rose and led Mrs. Brenton out of the room.

After they had left Arsenault said to Windflower, "Not bad. I like your interviewing style. In charge but cooperative. The only suggestion I would make is to sometimes let the silence linger a little more. You'd be surprised what people tell you when you let them sit in that for a while. They're much more nervous than you are. Otherwise you did great. "Let's wait until Ford gets back and we'll do a debrief."

"Thanks, Inspector," said Windflower. "I'm grateful for the chance to practice. You don't get too much opportunity for it in a small detachment."

"Maybe you should think about moving somewhere bigger," said Arsenault. "I think you have potential in investigations."

Then Ford came back into the room. "She's probably already on the line to her lawyer," he said.

"If it's the same one as her husband used we'll have our hands full," said Windflower.

"Who's that?" asked Ford.

"Donald Delaney," said Windflower.

"We are well aware of Mr. Delaney," said Arsenault. "Voice of the downtrodden and ill-used by the criminal justice system."

"As long as you have the moolah to pay up," added Ford.

"Well, let's just do our job, gentlemen," said Arsenault. "The justice system will work itself out."

"So what did you think about Marge Brenton's interview, Fordy?" asked Arsenault.

"I thought she was lying through her teeth," said Ford. "There's some kind of scam going on here but I can't figure out who's doing what to whom yet. Marge Brenton is claiming she did it and that it was an accident. Good story, but I don't believe her."

"Windflower?" asked Arsenault.

"I agree, sir. She's lying. Once we get forensics we'll have a better idea of who shot the gun. And I guess we should get an x-ray of her arm to see if it was even possible for her to do it."

"Good idea," said Arsenault. "Fordy, can you make that happen before her lawyer gets here. He might not readily agree with our approach."

"Also I tend to agree with both your observations. We don't have the whole story yet. Let's see what Sheridan has to say. But she is lying, that's for sure. But why? That's the real question. Once we figure that out we will be on the right track," said Arsenault. "Let's go see what young Mr. Sheridan has to say for himself after a night in jail."

Chapter Forty-Seven

James Sheridan looked much the worse for wear after a night in the Marystown jail. He looked fidgety and anxious and was biting his nails when the three Mounties strode into the room.

"James," said Windflower this is Inspector Arsenault and Staff Sergeant Ford. We want to ask you some questions."

Sheridan just blinked so Windflower continued. "Can you tell us what happened yesterday morning at the Brenton's house? First of all why were you there?"

"I went there to see Marge, Mrs. Brenton, before I left to go back home. I wanted to persuade her to leave that miserable son of a bitch and to come back to Ontario with me. She didn't have to live like that anymore. He was an animal," said Sheridan.

"Did you know that Harvey Brenton was suspected of being involved with your uncle's death?" asked Windflower.

"Suspected? That's a joke," said Sheridan. "Everyone around here knew what he was capable of and nobody did a damn thing about it. He got what he deserved."

"So what happened yesterday morning?" asked Windflower.

"As I said I went to see Marge but Harvey came home unexpected. He went after Marge again and I tried to stop him but he was too strong for me. I ran downstairs to look for a baseball bat but I found his shotgun instead. When I came back up he had a hold of Marge. I told him to back away and pointed the gun at him. He came towards me and I guess the gun just went off. It was an accident," said James Sheridan.

Windflower decided to shift gears. "Do you know that Marge Brenton has also confessed to killing Harvey Brenton? We've got her in a cell down the hall?

With this news James Sheridan jumped up and started at Windflower, screaming "Let her go, let her go!!", but he was restrained by Staff Sergeant Ford who sat him back down and held him.

"Yes," said Arsenault. "She's willing to take the fall for you. Or maybe you are taking the fall for her. We're getting confused, Mr. Sheridan. Which is it?"

"I told you," said Sheridan, "It was me. I am responsible. You have to let her go. Please." At this point Sheridan looked as if he was going to cry.

"We're not letting anyone go until we get to the bottom of this," said Windflower. "And once we get the forensics back we'll know which one of you actually shot Harvey Brenton. So you can make it easier on yourself by just telling us the truth now. We know all about your manslaughter case, James. Things are not going to go well for you unless you fess up now."

"Go to hell," said Sheridan. "You aren't trying to help me. I'm done talking. I want a lawyer."

"Ford, take Mr. Sheridan back to his cell. And arrange for him to make his call," said Arsenault.

After Ford and Sheridan left Arsenault said sarcastically, "I think that went well."

"Yeah," said Windflower. "Two indignant liars."

"It's a pretty clever plot, though," said Arsenault as Ford came back into the interview room. "It's interesting that both claim it was an accident. Windflower, did Harvey Brenton have a cell phone on him when he was found?"

"I don't know, but I can find out when I talk to Tizzard. Why do you want to know?" asked Windflower.

"Because if there's a phone call from his house to Mr. Brenton after around 9:45 yesterday morning, it will mean that he was invited back and didn't just come back on his own."

"And that means it wouldn't be an accident," said Windflower.

"Exactly. I guess we have a couple of hours before the lawyers are banging on our doors asking for their clients to be released. I can probably hold them off until court opens tomorrow morning, but that's it. So we have to figure out who to charge with what by then," said Arsenault.

"Get cracking on the forensics, Windflower. We need to know who fired the gun. And Fordy, get that lady x-rayed will you? We need to know if she could have fired that gun."

"Okay, I'm on it," said Windflower.

"Let's meet back here at 5 pm when the lady from the café in Grand Bank shows up. Okay?" asked Arsenault.

Both officers nodded and Windflower headed outside to get some fresh air and to call his home office. Hopefully Tizzard had some good news for him by now.

Windflower checked his cell phone and noticed there were three missed calls from Tizzard. He didn't bother checking his messages, just called him directly.

"Hey, Sarge," said Tizzard.

"Tizzard, what have you got for me?" asked Windflower.

"Well, I'm not sure the forensics will help us too much," said Tizzard. "On the fingerprints, both Marge Brenton and James Sheridan have their finger prints on the shotgun. But both also showed traces of powder residue on their hands."

"That means that both handled the gun," said Windflower. 'but it doesn't exactly narrow the field, does it?" he said.

"No, I guess not," said Tizzard. "On the other hand it means that one of them for sure killed Harvey Brenton."

"Or both," said Tizzard. "We looking into the conspiracy theory."

"Interesting," said Tizzard. I do have more substantive information on James Sheridan, though."

"Spill the beans," said Windflower.

"James Sheridan killed a classmate at community college in Brampton in 2005. Shot him in the chest with a sawed-off shotgun. Claimed it was an accident. Because he was found criminally not responsible his file is sealed under the Mental Health Act but the OPP guys were happy to share the information. They thought it was a cold blooded act that Sheridan got away with by playing a mental patient," said Tizzard.

"Anything else?" asked Windflower.

"A lot more," said Tizzard. "Part of Tizzard's defense was that he was abandoned by his mother when he was very small and was adopted by Georgette Sheridan."

"What's so interesting about that?" asked Windflower.

"Sheridan was born in Newfoundland. And when I went back through the records he was born at St. Clares Hospital in St. John's."

"James Elias Martin," said Windflower.

"What did you say?" asked Tizzard.

Windflower repeated it out loud. "Elias Martin is not James Sheridan's uncle," said Windflower. "He's his father."

"And his mother is," and Tizzard paused... "Marge Brenton. Wow."

"Okay, now things are starting to make some more sense," said Windflower. "I will pass our theory on to Inspector Arsenault. In the meantime, Tizzard, mum's the word."

"Got it, Boss," said Tizzard. "Anything else?"

"Yeah," said Windflower. "Did Harvey Brenton have a cell phone on him when he died?"

"Yes," said Tizzard. "A fancy new smart phone. Why?"

"I want you to check the phone and see where and when the last call to that cell phone was received."

"No problem," said Tizzard. "It's in the evidence room. I'll go and check it when we finish up here."

"And how's everything else going?" asked Windflower.

"Getting back to normal," said Tizzard. "If it's okay with you I am going to send the Marystown guys back tomorrow. We can handle our own patch now," he said.

"Oh, yeah and the Mayor was here. I told him that you had some ideas to talk to him about when you get back. That seemed to mollify him. At least he went away," said Tizzard.

"Great," laughed Windflower. "You've learned the number one trick of municipal policing, how to make the politicians disappear. I'll talk to you soon."

Then Windflower phoned Sheila to make sure that she and Marie were still on for 5 o'clock, but she had left the café for the day. Hopefully she was on her way. Windflower went back inside and briefed Arsenault and Ford on the latest intel and then walked with Ford to Timmy's for his third visit of the day. A man, especially a policeman, could get hooked on this, he thought.

Chapter Forty-Eight

As they waited for Sheila and Marie to come the three police colleagues shared a few stories about different cases in their career. Windflower talked a bit about his work in Halifax at the airport and both Arsenault and Ford shared a few humourous stories about life in major investigations in Montreal. By the time they were told that Marie and Sheila had arrived they were all in a more jovial mood.

The trio went down to the interview room where Sheila was trying to calm down a very nervous Marie. "It's only Sergeant Windflower and his friends," Sheila was overheard saying. "And you know him. He's in the Mug-Up every day."

"Hello Marie", said Windflower. "Hi Sheila."

Sheila smiled and Marie whispered a shy "Hello."

"These are my friends, Inspector Arsenault and Staff Sergeant Ford. Gentlemen let me introduce Sheila Hillier and Marie Baggs." said Windflower.

Sheila rose to greet the new men, "Pleased to meet you," she said to both.

"My pleasure," said Arsenault while Ford just smiled and shook her hand.

"Marie works at the café, the Mug-Up in Grand Bank," said Windflower, "and Sheila is the owner/manager."

"Thanks very much for coming Marie. Would you be more comfortable if Sheila stayed in here with you?" asked Windflower sensing the older woman's nervousness.

"That would be good," said Marie. "I've never been in jail before."

"Well, you're not really in jail right now," said Windflower. "You're kind of like just visiting, like the Monopoly game."

That statement had the effect of producing a weak smile in Marie so Windflower thought it best to proceed as quickly as possible to the interview.

"So Marie, we'd like to talk to you about what you might have seen or heard at the café the other day when Marge Brenton and the young man, James Sheridan were in there together. Do you remember that day?" Windflower asked.

"Yes, Sergeant," said Marie. "That was the last day before my two days off. I work three days on and then get two days off. Except during the summer when it's busy. Then I only get one day off at a time. You get run off your feet with them tourists you know," she said.

"Now on that day in question, when did Marge Brenton and her young friend come into the café?" Windflower asked.

"It was just after lunch," said Marie. "The big lunch crowd had gone and I was trying to clean up. She had a cup of tea and a raisin bun and he had a turkey sandwich with dressing," looking at Sheila for confirmation that she was doing okay as she answered. Shelia smiled so she continued, "I asked them if they wanted dessert but they said no so I kept working around them."

"What were they talking about?" asked Windflower and it felt like the other two officers leant in towards Marie as she thought about her answer.

"Well, I think they were talking about 'himself', said Marie.

"Himself?" asked Windflower.

"The late Mr. Harvey Brenton," said Marie and she made the sign of the cross as she said his name.

"And what were they talking about exactly?" asked Windflower.

"Well, I couldn't say exactly," said Marie. "Whenever I came close they would lower their voices, but I am a good listener."

"I bet you are," said Windflower. "So to the best of your ability can you tell us what you heard?"

"They never said his name," she continued, blessing herself again, "but I did hear them talking about the best place to get rid of something. He said to bury it but she said that the ocean was the best place if you wanted to make sure that it would never be found again."

"At the end he agreed with Marge Brenton and said I don't care what happens but I want to make sure that no one ever sees 'him' again. That's when I knew they were talking about a somebody and not a something," concluded Marie.

"I didn't clue into it right away," said Marie. "You hear so many things. You wouldn't believe the things I've heard at the Mug-Up." At this Marie started to glow a bright pink but Sheila reached over and gave her hand a welcome squeeze.

"I'm sure you do, Marie. Is there anything else you remember about that day or that conversation?" asked Windflower.

"Yes. After we heard the terrible news," she added, once again blessing herself as if to ward off any evil spirits, "I started thinking about it and I remembered that just before they left he said 'I'll be there about 9:30 and we'll call him then.' Then he reached over and gave her a kiss on the cheek and said 'I love you'. You never forget something like that. It was very touching."

"It sounds like it was," said Windflower. "I think we're done. Anybody have any other questions?" he asked of Arsenault and Ford but both simply shook their heads.

"Well thank you so much, Marie," said Windflower. "You've been a great help."

"My pleasure," said Marie, feeling and looking quite pleased with herself and her performance.

"I will see our guests out," said Windflower as he led the two ladies out of the room and back to the front entrance.

"Thanks again, Marie," said Windflower as he walked them to Sheila's car. "If you go over to the restaurant at the Marystown Motel I will be over as soon as I can," said Windflower.

He waited until they pulled out of the parking lot and then went back into the interview room with Arsenault and Ford.

"Well, gentlemen, what do you think?" asked Arsenault. "We're going to have to make recommendations on charges by tomorrow morning. I've got a call from Marge Brenton's lawyer, Mr. Delaney that I haven't returned but I expect that he will be at the courthouse bright and early tomorrow morning seeking the release of his client. And I expect James Sheridan's lawyer to be close behind."

"Well, I think it's clear that both of them were in on it and if I were a betting man I would bet on Sheridan as the shooter," said Ford.

"I don't disagree," said Windflower. "If Marge Brenton's arm is broken then she probably couldn't have done it and if we were to charge her she would likely claim that in court."

"On the other hand we will likely have difficulty bringing James Sheridan's past record into the case," said Ford. "I'm not sure what the rules are on that."

"I think that it will be difficult but not impossible to prove a conspiracy," said Windflower, "especially if we have a phone call to Harvey Brenton from his residence that morning."

"Those are all useful points," said Arsenault, "but since none of us are lawyers I suggest we schedule a meeting with the Crown Attorney tomorrow morning at 9. Get a good sleep, gentlemen and bring your best brains to work tomorrow morning."

Both of the other men nodded and said goodnight to the Inspector. Ford offered to buy Windflower a beer on the way home but Windflower explained that he had dinner plans.

"Is that your lady?" asked Ford, inquiring about Sheila. "She's a good looking woman, Sergeant."

"Yeah, we just started seeing each other," said Windflower. "I think she's pretty special."

"I think so too," said Ford. "Do you want a lift to the hotel? I'm going right by there."

"Sure, that would be great," said Windflower and jumped into Ford's F-150 pickup. "Nice wheels," he said.

"Yeah, get's me around," said Ford. "I can throw my ATV in the back for hunting season and just head for the back woods. You'll have to come back in the fall. I've got a little cabin just on a lake. It's absolutely gorgeous back there."

"I'd like that," said Windflower as he got out in front of the hotel. "See you tomorrow." Ford waved goodbye and was soon gone down the road towards home.

Chapter Forty-Nine

Windflower went into the restaurant and found Marie and Sheila in a comfortable booth in the window. They already had drinks, Sheila with what looked like an iced tea and Marie with a Coke. Windflower sat down and motioned the waitress over. "I'll have one of those," he said pointing to Sheila's drink.

"I thought you might be looking for something a little stronger," said Sheila.

"I'd like it," said Windflower, "but I'm still on duty."

"Let's have a look at the menu," he said. "I hope you're hungry, Marie."

"I'm starved," said Marie. "I couldn't eat anything before I came over to do this. I was too anxious."

"Well, it's over and you did great," said Sheila.

"Ok, everybody ready?" asked Windflower as the waitress returned with his tea. Windflower ordered the seafood chowder along with Marie as a starter while Sheila asked for a Caesar salad. For their mains Marie had pan fried cod with scrunchions, tasty little bits of pork fried to a crisp, Sheila had blackened salmon and Windflower ordered the fisherman's platter.

Soon they were enjoying their appetizers and making small talk about the café and its crew of unusual customers. Marie was surprisingly funny as she mimicked some of their more outrageous antics. Windflower hadn't had such a good laugh since forever and from time to time caught Sheila's eye and they shared a pleasant smile together.

When their main courses arrived they were all surprised by the mounds of food that came with their orders. Windflower had an especially large plate of pan fried cod plus grilled salmon, sautéed shrimp and scallops. Marie reminded him that he could always take home what he couldn't eat but at the end that wasn't necessary. Everyone cleaned their plates and sat there just looking completely stuffed and satisfied. No one had room for dessert but Windflower offered them a cup of coffee at Tim Horton's for the road and the ladies gladly accepted.

Marie went to the washroom while Windflower and Sheila stood in line for coffee and they at least had a couple of private moments to connect.

"Are you okay?" asked Sheila. "Sometimes you look as if you're a million miles away."

"Yes, just thinking about the case," said Windflower. "I guess the good news is that our part is coming to an end. We meet with the Crown Attorney tomorrow morning and then it's in their hands."

"Good," said Sheila, as Marie returned, "I can't wait to have you to myself for a while."

Windflower got their coffees and wished them both a safe journey home. He went up to his room and decided to check in with Tizzard. Once again when he checked his phone there were three more calls from Tizzard. That boy is sure excitable, thought Windflower.

"Boss, I've been trying to call you," said Tizzard.

"Well, you got me now," said Windflower. "What's up?"

"There's a message on Brenton's phone, just like you thought. 10:25 a.m. from Brenton's home phone. So they called him to come home," said Tizzard.

"Well, one of them called him," said Windflower. "But that would kind of rule out an accident, don't you think?"

"I agree," said Tizzard. "So who is going to be charged?" he asked.

"Not completely sure yet. Certainly Sheridan. It looks like he fired the gun. We meet with the CA tomorrow morning to decide the rest," said Windflower.

"Wow, wouldn't it be something if either one of them got away with this?" asked Tizzard.

"Yeah, I know," said Windflower. "Well we'll do the best we can and then it's up to lawyers and judges," said Windflower.

"That's a scary thought," said Tizzard. "But you know, Boss, I think we did a pretty good job on our end."

"I do too, Tizzard. I do too," said Windflower as he hung up.

Windflower tried to read or watch TV but had no success in getting his mind off the matters at hand. As he worked his way back through things he settled on Georgette Sheridan. That's one person who knows a lot more than she's let on so far. Maybe she can tell me something else, he thought.

He found her number in his address book and called her home in Ontario.

"Hello," came the familiar woman's voice.

"Mrs. Sheridan, it's Sergeant Winston Windflower from Grand Bank," he said.

"Do you have news about James?" she asked. "I spoke to the lawyer a little while ago and he said James might have been involved in Harvey Brenton's death. Is that true?"

"Well, I did want to talk to you about James, Mrs. Sheridan. He is under investigation so I can't say a lot about that right now. We should know more about that in the next few days. What I really want to know about are James' early years. We've figured out who his mother and father are, Mrs. Sheridan."

She sighed. "I guess I knew that would come out sooner or later. But I did manage to keep it from James, right up until Elias died. Then I felt that I had to tell him. Poor James, he didn't even know he was adopted. I hope my telling him didn't bring all this trouble on him. I feel so responsible," said Georgette Sheridan.

"You are not responsible for his actions," said Windflower. "Your son," he began and then deliberately pausing, "James, is 27 years old."

"I know but I have had him with me since he was just a month old. For Marge and Elias to get together was a terrible mistake but I guess that they couldn't stop themselves. They had both been married for a while when they started getting together, innocently at first, and then, well you know," said Georgette Sheridan.

"After Marge got pregnant she called me in a panic. My first suggestion was to try and pass the baby off as Harvey's, but that wouldn't work. Harvey had lost interest in Marge in that way by then. He had his kids and decided he didn't want anymore so he had a vasectomy. He pursued other interests in regards to sex, if you know what I mean," she continued.

231

"So at the end she had to tell Harvey and he made her tell him who the father was. That's when the beatings started and Marge never said anything about them because she felt guilty. Once Harvey's rage died down he agreed that Marge could go away and have the baby in St. John's and then my husband and I would adopt the child. Harvey managed to smooth the way through the adoption agency in Newfoundland and we formally adopted James about a month after his birth." she said.

There was a long silence and then a sigh.

"Go on, Mrs. Sheridan," said Windflower softly.

"His only conditions were that the child could never be told who his mother and father were and that the child be kept away from Grand Bank. For my part I kept my end of the bargain except that when James got a bit bigger I started bringing him to Grand Bank. I would arrange it when I knew Harvey and Marge would be away and Elias was sworn to secrecy not to reveal his identity to James. At least this way both of them got to see each other, even if they weren't known to each other as father and son," said Georgette Sheridan.

"That was a nice thing to do, for both of them," said Windflower sincerely.

"I thought so," she said. "But I wish I had never told him about his dad."

"What about James' other incident?" asked Windflower.

"I'm not talking about that," said Georgette Sheridan. "That was long ago and James was sick then. I probably shouldn't have told you anything. You're not going to help James. You're trying to put him in jail." With that Windflower heard the phone click and the line went dead.

Well at least I know the real story now, thought Windflower. He pulled out his book and started to read. About a hundred pages later he turned out the lights and fell into bed.

Surprisingly he fell asleep almost immediately and didn't wake until his morning wake up call from the front desk.

Chapter Fifty

Windflower showered and shaved and after a quick breakfast in the hotel restaurant was on his way to the Marystown detachment at a brisk pace. A pickup slowed next to him and he recognized Ford as the driver. "Hop in," said Ford.

The two Mounties strode into the building together and went up to Inspector Arsenault's office. Louise was deftly directing traffic in person and on the phone but managed to say good morning and to note to Windflower that she had an expense check ready for him along with the forms and that he could just leave his room key at the desk on the way out of his hotel. "As long as you don't have any incidentals," she said. That means a bar bill, thought Windflower, who simply nodded at the directions and the obvious news that he was going home sooner than he thought.

As they were waiting in the reception area outside Arsenault's office a young man dressed in a Brooks Brothers suit and wearing Italian loafers marched into the room and smiled good morning to Louise who stopped the many things she was doing to respond. Windflower looked at Ford who mouthed "It's the CA".

After being ignored for a few minutes Ford stood up and said good morning to the Crown Attorney. The CA shook his hand briefly and looked at Windflower who had his hand extended.

"Wallace Winters." He smiled at Windflower. "You must be the Grand Bank guy."

"Winston Windflower," he replied.

"Where are we, Louise, is he coming?" Winters asked, pointing towards the door.

"It's the big conference room," said Louise. "There should be coffee. I'll send him right over."

The two policemen and the lawyer walked to the conference room down the hall and got them selves a coffee and just settled in when Inspector Arsenault arrived.

"Okay, let's get going," said Winters. "I've got them put off until 11:30 but with or without me the judge will hear applications for release of Mrs. Brenton and Sheridan. So what can you tell me?" he asked.

"Windflower, why don't you take the lead and walk Winters through the Elias Martin case and then up to Harvey Brenton's death. Fordy, you can bring us up to date on what's happened here in the last few days," said Arsenault.

Windflower and Ford went through all the details including Windflower's conversation with Georgette Sheridan and Ford's confirmation from the hospital that Marge Brenton's wrist was broken in two places, making it practically impossible for her to hold and shoot the shotgun.

An hour and a half later Winters had twelve pages of a legal size pad filled with notes. "You guys are thorough," he said. "So what's your recommendation?"

Arsenault looked at his team and said, "We think that James Sheridan pulled the trigger and should be charged with pre-mediated murder. We know that Marge Brenton was involved but we are not sure what if anything she should or could be charged with," said Arsenault. "Why don't you give us some options and the chances of conviction?"

"Well the chances of conviction are always fifty-fifty," said Winters. "Especially if we get in front of a jury. But based on what you told me I would feel good about presenting on James Sheridan. Even if we can't use his previous conviction, which I'm not sure we can't, we have his fingerprints on the gun and his obvious motive. Harvey Brenton killed his father."

"On Marge Brenton it is a little more dicey," Winters added. "We could charge her with a lot of things. But getting a conviction, now that's a different story."

"Our options range from trying to make a murder charge, some form of conspiracy charge, or being an accessory to murder, or even interfering with a criminal investigation because she lied with her confession. But every possibility has its own difficulties. Whatever we might charge her with today, she is going to get bail and will be out by this afternoon. And then her lawyer, who I think will be Delaney, will have all the time in the world to fashion a case," concluded Winters.

"And I didn't even get into the politics of charging a battered woman with any kind of crime against her husband. Every woman's group on the Southeast coast will be protesting outside the courtroom," he added.

"But we can't just let her walk away scot-free, can we?" asked Windflower.

The other three men just looked at him and sighed warily.

"There is another option," said Winters. "And that is to negotiate a plea for a lesser offense with Mrs. Brenton's lawyer. It would probably mean no jail time but it would be a conviction and clears the field for a better chance of convicting Sheridan."

"But she won't testify against her own son, will she Windflower?" asked Arsenault.

"Not a chance," said Windflower.

"She doesn't have to," said Winters. "She just has to stay quiet and not lie for him. That would be enough to break their pact. And it would be enough for a conviction."

"It's not ideal, but it may be the best we can hope for," said Arsenault. "The question is can we live with it?"

Windflower realized that all eyes in the room were on him and he felt uncomfortably warm. "I don't really understand how all this works," he said, "but if you are telling me that this is the best we can do, I can live with it. In my mind Elias Martin has gotten his justice and even Harvey Brenton can have his this way too."

"So, I'm going to charge James Sheridan and then talk to Delaney about Marge Brenton," said Winters. "Thank you, gentlemen," he said as he packed up his papers and left the room.

"Fordy, can you leave us alone for a minute," said Inspector Arsenault after Winters had gone. Ford left and Arsenault turned to Windflower.

"You did a good job here Sergeant," said Arsenault. "We may not have gotten everything but we did okay. Sheridan will probably try his mental illness scenario on again but I don't think it will sell this time. Harvey Brenton might have been a mean bastard but he has a right to justice too. And Marge Brenton may not be going to jail but her son is and she will have a hard time getting over what has happened to her."

"You're right," said Windflower. "Even though I've been a cop for a long time I am always surprised how ineffective the justice system really is. But I guess we do what we can. And for today, that will have to be good enough."

"You're a good man, and a good policeman," said Arsenault. "Just because we don't get the result we want doesn't mean we give up trying. Keep at it, Windflower."

"And I meant what I said to you the other day. You've got a bright future in investigations if you're interested. In fact I can probably make a space for you here in Marystown if you want to transfer over," said the Inspector.

"Thanks for the offer, Inspector, but I think I'm looking forward to a couple of more years in sleepy Grand Bank. I think the pace suits me better. But if you ever need an extra hand on an investigation I'd be happy to come over for a few days," said Windflower.

"That's a deal, then," said Arsenault. "I'm going to enjoy working with you, Windflower."

"I am too," said Windflower.

After checking out of his room and leaving the room key at the front desk as directed Windflower went to his car and started the trip back to Grand Bank. One more coffee at Timmy's he thought and pulled up to the drive through. When he was passing by he saw Staff Sergeant Ford in the window and waved goodbye.

As he watched the beautiful natural beauty of Marystown harbour fade in his rear view mirror he thought, man, will it ever be nice to be back in Grand Bank again.

Epilogue

Two weeks later Windflower was sitting with Howard Stoodley pretending to go through Stoodley's latest work while Sheila and Moira chatted and cleaned up the last of the dishes. All of the other guests had left so they had a chance to catch up on the latest happenings.

"That was a wonderful Jiggs Dinner," said Windflower having just devoured his share of the traditional Newfoundland feast. "Sorry I had to delay accepting your invitation for so long. Been busy, you know. But that was a great meal."

"Well, you can thank Moira for that," said Stoodley. "I'd starve on my own. I hear Sheila is pretty handy in the kitchen too."

"She is indeed," said Windflower. "I'll see if I can get her to agree to a return engagement."

"Engagement, now that's an interesting word," laughed Stoodley, "a little Freudian slip, Winston?"

"One step at a time, Howard," replied Windflower. "If such an unlikely event should ever happen you'll be the first to know."

"I heard from Herb that the investigation is going quite well. It looks like MacIntosh has been given an ultimatum. Take retirement or lose his pension," said Stoodley.

'He'll take his pension. He's a greedy bastard," said Windflower. "And good riddance to him. I really like his replacement, Kevin Arsenault."

"Yeah, I've heard good things about him too," said Stoodley. "And young Sheridan pleaded guilty to second-degree murder I see. He's going to be sentenced next week."

"That is good news," said Windflower. "You know maybe I shouldn't but I kind of feel sorry for Marge Brenton in all of this. She finally gets reunited with her son and now he's gone to prison for as long as she'll live."

"The whole thing is a bit tragic," said Stoodley. "But on to more important things, I hear that the Mayor and the Mounties are spearheading a drive to get the youth centre back up and running. Congratulations."

"It's actually Fortier and Corporal Tizzard who are spearheading that effort. I just smoothed the way for the Mayor to take credit and launch his re-election bid," said Windflower.

"You keep this up and you might have a future in politics yourself," said Stoodley.

"Not a chance," said Windflower. "I'm just a humble policeman trying to serve the community."

"Now I'm convinced of it," laughed Stoodley.

Both men laughed and went to see their better halves for a cup of tea and maybe even a hand of cards before they called it a night.

The End

About the Author

Mike Martin was born in Newfoundland on the East Coast of Canada and now lives and works in Ottawa, Ontario. He is a longtime freelance writer and his articles and essays have appeared in newspapers, magazines and online across Canada as well as in the United States and New Zealand. He is the author of "Change the Things You Can: Dealing with Difficult People and has written a number of short stories that have published in various publications including Canadian Stories and Downhome magazine. The Walker on the Cape is his first full fiction book and the premiere of the Winston Windflower mystery series.

He is a member of Ottawa Independent Writers, Capital Crime Writers, the Crime Writers of Canada and the Newfoundland Writers' Guild.

For more information and to comment on this book please visit: www.walkeronthecape.com